The
Crimson
Oak

THE
CRIMSON
OAK

E.M. Almedingen

Coward-McCann, Inc.
New York

Designed by Charlotte Staub

First printing
Printed in the United States of America
First published by Methuen Children's Books, Ltd.

Library of Congress Cataloging in Publication Data
Almedingen, E. M. (Edith Martha), 1898-1971.
The crimson oak.
Summary: Peter, a Russian peasant boy, twelve
years old in the year 1739 and full of dreams, chances
to cross paths with the exiled Princess Elizabeth
and comes to realize his fate is linked to hers.
1. Soviet Union—History—1689-1800—Juvenile
fiction. 2. Elizabeth, Empress of Russia, 1709-
1762—Juvenile fiction. [1. Soviet Union—History
—Fiction. 2. Elizabeth, Empress of Russia,
1709-1762—Fiction] I. Title.
PZ7.A446Cr 1981   [Fic]   82-12556
ISBN 0-698-20569-3

CONTENTS

The
Crimson
Oak

I What happened to Peter in Makar's Wood

I t fell on a day in the summer of 1739, though Peter, peasant's son that he was, would not have known either the year or the month. What he did know was that the hay harvest lay behind him, that Elijah the prophet had his chariot safely away in the heavenly coachhouse since no thunderstorms had troubled the neighborhood for a long time, that the peas were swelling and the turnips promised well, and that the woods were rich with wild berries.

Finally, he woke on that particular morning, aware that a whole day's holiday lay before him.

3

No chopping of wood, no cleaning of byres or hens' houses, no journeys to the river to fetch water in those wooden buckets which were so easy to carry down to the bank and so difficult to bring home.

A day's holiday! At that time, in Russia, a peasant boy was lucky if he got two such days in the year!

Peter's gray eyes were shining. There was sun in his thoughts, and the fact that he had made no definite plans for the day added to the delight. If you did not know just what you were going to do, he said to himself, anything might happen. He might, if he wished, slip down to the little wooden church and look once again at the heavily bound service books, their pages covered with those tantalizing strokes and curves in black which meant something to the deacon and nothing at all to him, Peter. Ah no, he said to himself, he would not go down to the church. It was no use spoiling the day in such a manner, no use brooding over the memory of the deacon's gruff voice saying to him, "Now then, my lad, I'll turn over one more page for you to stare at and that's enough. Books are not for the likes of you, see? Your job is to work in the fields, peasant's son that you are."

Peter shook his tousled flaxen head and finished the last drop of milk in his mug. Well, then, there were the meadows, the wood, and the river—the whole of his little world to lose himself in till sunset, truly a blessed day which came so seldom that Peter could not remember when he had last had one.

Here he saw his mother stand by the table, two big baskets in her hands. He got up, wiped his mouth with the back of his hand, and smiled shyly.

"Enjoy yourself, lad," Marfa smiled back at him. "I reckon you are going to make for the woods. Well, wild raspberries will be at their best, and it's time we had a raspberry pie."

At once the light went out of Peter's eyes. Here was a plan thrust on him. Here also was a task. The sun streamed into the bare little hut, but its walls were darkened for him.

"Oh, Mama," he began, the thin shoulders drooping under the rough gray smock. "I meant—I wanted—" He gulped hard and stood silent.

"Well, you like your raspberry pie," Marfa said not unkindly, "and here is your dinner, lad." She pointed at a satchel lying in one of the baskets and paused, her brown deeply wrinkled face still smiling. "God's own weather for you, too! Going all by yourself, are you, or with little Mashka? Her mother won't let her go alone into the woods," added Marfa conversationally.

"I am going alone," Peter muttered, stretched two grubby, bony hands for the baskets, and ran out of the little hut.

He supposed he would have to get the raspberries, but he did not see why he should endure the company of Mashka, ten to his twelve, a little girl who was afraid of adders and spiders, and burst into tears at the very first nettle sting.

His bare feet in the thick gray-yellow dust outside the door, Peter paused for a quick look up and down the curving street of the village. Mashka's

5

faded red kerchief was not to be seen anywhere. Peter sighed in relief, turned, and ran as fast as his spindly legs would carry him. The twin rows of low-humped roofs, with no chimneys to them, were left behind in about two minutes. Beyond a huddle of shippons and byres, held in common by the villagers, stretched the fields of rye, oats, and barley. Far ahead lay the deep dark-green mass of the woods, the river curving at their foot. There was a scent of mown hay and bruised grass in the air. The vast gray-green and honey-golden fields, lavishly embroidered with poppy and cornflower, shimmered in the late June sunlight. Far above, a lark, all but lost to sight, was singing. Below, among the tall grasses by the field edge grasshoppers were buzzing, and on the common, cattle moved leisurely from clump to clump of grass, their chestnut-brown flanks satin under the sun.

It seemed a spacious enough world, all of it so familiar to Peter that he raced along without seeing much of it. Raspberries grew apace in Makar's Wood—some distance from the village, but the wood was edged by a stream. He would eat his dinner there, Peter decided, before he began picking the berries. He stopped, put both baskets on the ground, and peered into the satchel. Its contents made him grin. Two large hunks of rye bread, a herring, and a piece of honeycake! It was certainly a holiday dinner and he felt heartened.

The sun stood high by the time Peter reached the outskirts of Makar's Wood just at the spot where the stream ran deep and wide enough to suggest a dip. Peter pulled off his tattered smock—he wore no other clothes—and leaped. The icy water made him shiver, but he plunged a second time, and then swam, his arms and legs threshing the water. It seemed good. But he was hungry and soon enough he jumped on the bank, his wet matted hair glinting almost like silver. He rolled on the grass to dry himself, then opened the satchel and ate slowly and contentedly. The last crumb finished—and certainly, the gingerbread tasted good—Peter knelt by the stream, cupped both hands, and quenched his thirst in several quick gulps.

"Now for the berries," he said aloud, picked up the baskets, and plunged into the wood.

Peter had a fairly clear idea where to look for the berries. True that a holiday came to him seldom enough, yet it happened that sometimes he would be sent to the common to drive back the cattle or to gather kindling in the thick tangle of undergrowth at its western end. Such errands made it possible for Peter to steal some time for himself, and to race through Makar's Wood right to its end, there to spend a few moments under the wide-boughed shade of an old crimson oak. It was not particularly beautiful; its gnarled arms, patchily covered by lichen, sprawled in all directions, and one or two of the limbs were withered through age, but to Peter that tree stood for warmth and freedom and an opportunity to think his secret thoughts in peace. He had no words to explain any of it. He just loved the tree.

Makar's Wood was nearly all elm and larch, with a willow and a stunted oak here and there. The crimson oak towered over them all. To sit under its shade was to be within an enchanted kingdom. Peter was friends with all the young people in the village, but he shared his secrets with none of them. They would have dismissed it for a piece of foolishness. What was there in an old tree, they would have laughed. So the secret remained Peter's own, as much his own as his deeply scratched feet and roughened bony hands.

Makar's Wood had quite a number of clearings, but a stranger would have easily lost his way in it. Not so Peter. He walked briskly on the needle-carpeted floor, bearing now right, now left, his accustomed eyes at home in the pale golden-green light. It did not take him very long to reach the spot where the dark green leafage was broken by the crimson enamel of the berries.

Peter ate several handfuls before he started filling the baskets. That done, he picked them up and was turning back when suddenly he heard a horse's loud whinny somewhere behind him. He turned and peered hard, but the trees were far too close together for him to see anything at all.

He stood rooted. Fear gripped him. He had never heard of anyone riding in Makar's Wood. It was probably a brigand. Brigands were known to kill people. Peter's teeth began to chatter, but still he would not move.

At that moment he heard the horse again, and the whinny was immediately followed by a woman's loud voice.

"Someone in trouble! There's that clearing to the left," remembered Peter and, clutching the baskets hard, he ran off in the direction of the noise.

He reached the clearing soon enough. No brigands were to be seen. The sun-dappled space, gay with lady's smock and cinquefoil, was something like a stage, with a young woman on horseback and a bear making toward her, his forepaws raised above his head. The horse reared, all but unseating the rider, and the bear moved closer.

"Hi, hi," shouted Peter, and the bear turned his head very slowly. Quick as lightning, Peter flung both baskets well away to the left. The bear growled, turned, and made for the crimson scatter of berries. Peter, breath all but failing him, ran across the glade.

"That will keep him busy, mistress," he panted, "and you ride away—"

"Jump up behind me," the woman ordered him.

Peter had never been on horseback, but within an instant there he was, clutching at the rider's waist. The horse galloped through the clearing. Peter's heart hammering, he closed his eyes. Was he awake? Was he dreaming? He could not tell. He heard the rider speak very gently to the mount, whose pace began slowing by degrees. A tree branch hit Peter's right cheek. Then he knew that the rider was reining in and he opened his eyes.

They had reached the northern edge of Makar's Wood, and there was the crimson oak.

"Jump down," the woman told him.

Peter obeyed, but he felt rather unsteady, and jumped so clumsily that he rolled down on the silken grass. The woman leaped out of the saddle, fondled the horse's neck for a moment, and then measured Peter with a searching look.

"You know the wood, don't you?"

"Yes, mistress," he replied huskily.

He felt confused and still frightened. He stood, his head bent.

"Ever met a bear there?"

"No mistress, but I have heard them sometimes, and I would run away—"

"Why?"

"Frightened of them, mistress," he gulped.

"Where do you live?" she flung at him abruptly.

"At Malinka, mistress—"

"Ah yes, I have heard of that village." Her voice fell to a lower key. "Bless you, boy! Do you know what you have done?"

Dumb, Peter shook his tousled head, but the lady was obviously waiting for an answer, and he mumbled shyly:

"Why, mistress, it came to my mind that bears like raspberries—"

"They do indeed," she said very softly, and Peter raised his head.

He understood all she said but he knew that she did not use the peasant speech. He wondered if she were some noble lady from Moscow, a place so full of wonders that some folk did not believe it existed. Peter dared ask no questions, but he stared hard. The horse was a magnificent, well-groomed chestnut, but the rider's green habit was shabby and it had clumsy patches here and there, and her hands were ungloved. Under a somewhat dusty black tricorne a beautiful face was smiling at Peter, but he felt very ill at ease. He wished he might run away. . . .

"Well, I'll take you to the outskirts of Malinka," said the lady. "We had better keep clear of the wood. Don't look so worried—I know the way round. Here, wait a moment," and she moved nearer to the oak and stretched up her right arm to one of the lower branches. Peter saw that the sleeve was torn at the shoulder.

"It is a good tree, mistress," he ventured, watching her break off a small twig.

"It is," she agreed, and her dark blue eyes considered the little twig for a moment. "What is your name, boy?"

"Peter, mistress, Peter Belov. My father is the elder at Malinka."

"I see," she said and handed him the twig. "Take it and keep it, and I'll tell you why when we get near your home. But I don't want you to tell anyone that you have met me. Promise?"

"Yes, mistress." Slowly and reverently Peter made the sign of the cross in token of his promise.

They rode along the edge of the wood and across one common and another. The lady kept silent and Peter dared not speak, but he took good care not to loosen his clutch on the little twig. At the top of a rye field she halted the horse, told Peter to jump down, and then bent toward him from the saddle.

"Now listen carefully," she said in her musical voice. "I am so poor now that I could not give you even a copper piece today. But I never forget any service done to me, and I hope the time may come when I shall be able to reward you. I want you to take great care of this twig. Do you understand?"

"Yes, mistress."

"At the right time you will come and bring this twig, and I'll give you the reward you've won today."

Peter grew suddenly bold.

"Where shall I see you, mistress? in Moscow, or will you come to Malinka? My mum can bake a fine cabbage pie when things are not hard with us."

The dark blue eyes were filled with laughter.

"Thank you, Peter. I'll remember. No, it may well be even further than Moscow—someday—"

"Ah but your name, mistress, your name—"

"My name?" For an instant a shadow fell across the lovely face and then she smiled again. "Well, now they all call me Princess Elizabeth. God bless you, lad—" She raised one ungloved hand and galloped away in a cloud of gray-golden dust.

Peter, mouth wide open, just stood and stared. "So that is what she is like!" he mumbled to the bruised grass at his feet. "Queen of heaven, I would not mind going hungry if that helped her!"

2 Another adventure knocks at Peter's door

Peter had never been away from his village. He could neither read nor write, but he had early learned to observe and to listen. He knew enough about Princess Elizabeth to realize the reason for her telling him not to mention their meeting in the wood. To talk about her was unsafe in those days. So Zakhar, Peter's father, would say on the very rare occasions when the lady's name came to be mentioned. Even when inside his own hut, Zakhar would look right and left as though he expected the very walls to charge him with high treason. And that was easily understood when you remembered that members of the Imperial secret police were always traveling up and down the country in search of conspiracies.

Those were very hard times for Russia. The great Tsar Peter had died in 1725, and his widow, crowned as Catherine I, had reigned a bare two years. Catherine had two daughters; the elder, Anna, was married to the Duke of Holstein, and the younger, Elizabeth, was still in her late teens at the time of her mother's death. In 1727 the crown went to a thirteen-year-old boy, Elizabeth's nephew, who died of smallpox in January 1730 on the eve of his wedding day. It then seemed that Elizabeth was the rightful heir, and the nation certainly expected her to succeed, but the sovereign's election rested with the Senate, and they chose to offer the crown to Tsar Peter's niece, Anna, the widowed Duchess of Courland.

With Anna's arrival in the early spring of 1730, all sorts of troubles fell upon the country. As Empress, she grew wildly extravagant, and the nation suffered because of the increased taxation. Then Anna, who had been surrounded by Germans for many years, brought quite a number of her favorites with her, and showered land, money, and fabulous jewels on them. In particular, there was one Johan Bihren, a man of very low origins. Anna was great friends with him and his wife. She created him Duke of Courland, and Bihren succeeded in convincing her that her life was in constant danger because of many malcontents who would have preferred to see Princess Elizabeth on the throne. Anna promptly had Elizabeth exiled to a poor manor in the neighborhood of Peter's village and reduced her allowance to a pittance. Next, she established her Secret Chancery "for the safeguarding of the Crown and the sovereign's person." Its slogan, "Word and Deed," was dreadful to hear. It meant immediate arrest, possibly torture, a parody of a trial with bribed witnesses to prove the guilt of an innocent person, and then execution.

Naturally, Peter did not know much about those matters in detail, but he knew enough to realize why he must not mention his meeting with the exiled princess. Even little humble Malinka, secluded though it was, could not consider itself safe from the tentacles of the Secret Chancery.

They were all serfs there but, the village being a crown manor, they belonged to the Crown and not to individual masters. That, however, did not make life any easier for the peasants; they were at the mercy of tax collectors who were supposed to come down twice a year. In reality, they came when it suited them, held their sessions in the priest's house, and fleeced everybody in the village. Peasants had no money, and all their taxes were paid in kind: dried fish, corn, root vegetables, berries, mushrooms, eggs, timber, and linen. All the amounts were fixed by law, but the collectors never failed to take advantage of the peasants' ignorance of the law and they varied the tribute as it pleased them.

Peter's father, Zakhar, was the elder at Malinka. The position carried no privileges. Rather, it was harder for him than for the others. Zakhar was held responsible for all the arrears. Many a time would

Peter crouch outside the priest's little house and cry as he heard sharp blows falling on his father's shoulders because one Ivan had failed to deliver the right measure of timber, or one Maria had forgotten to keep her tally of eggs.

For all of them, it was a life woven of one hardship after another. When quite small, Peter would be up before dawn in the summer to help his father in the fields. The working day ended at sunset, and hay and corn harvests were spells of backbreaking toil. The pace slackened in the autumn. With the first frosts, cattle would be driven into the great communal byres and poultry brought into the huts. These had no chimneys and were so full of smoke that often doors had to be opened to clear the air.

For all their unceasing work they were desperately poor. At Peter's, there was just one pair of boots for the three of them.

His home was built of roughly hacked wooden planks held together by pitch and boiled moss. There was just one room. The floor was earthen, and the tiny window had a piece of ox bladder stretched across it. For furniture there was a table, a trestle, and a shelf for a few pots and pans. Most of the space was taken by a large stove, whose flat top served as a bed for Peter's parents. He slept on the floor, on a rough pallet—or mat—made from a few armfuls of hay covered by a worn-out horsecloth.

But Peter had never known any other conditions. Hardships, as such, never troubled him, and each of the four seasons brought its own excitements. He preferred spring to all the others. However hard the work, it was good to run about again, to watch green life returning to tree and bush, to see the river freed of ice, and to wait for the thrush's song.

Only when Peter got almost in sight of the village did he remember his mother's baskets left behind in Makar's Wood. Their loss certainly meant a beating . . . Ah well—he tossed back a lock of flaxen hair and ran a little faster. He did not really mind the beating, but he must be careful about the story he would tell. Certainly, he might mention the bear. Anyone would run on seeing a bear, thought Peter.

Here he stopped. He saw three barrel-shaped green carts outside the priest's house and quite a crowd milling up and down the village street. From where he stood, he could hear the shrill wailing of the women. There was no doubt about it: the tax collectors were paying one of their unexpected visits to Malinka.

"Poor old Dad," thought Peter. "What with the bees failing and that hen sickness, there is sure to be trouble . . ."

He turned sharply and reached the village from the back. He felt pretty sure that his mother would be out, and there was one urgent job he must do: put the crimson oak twig into safety.

Just behind the hut ran an oblong patch of ground where carrots and turnips were grown every summer. At its end, half-screened by tangled, overgrown bear-berry bushes, stood a tumbledown shed where, in incredibly remote days, Zakhar had kept the only horse he had ever had. The animal had long since gone. The shed remained, and Peter had secretly dug a hole in its farthest, darkest corner. In that hole, carefully covered up by soil and dead leaves, he kept a small iron box once found by him on the river bank. Inside the box were a knife with a bone handle and a large copper coin flung at him by an officer, whose horse Peter had once minded for the space of an hour. He was vague about the value of the coin, but it was big and heavy, and he imagined himself very rich every time he looked at it.

It did not take him long to hide the little twig. He stared at it for quite a minute before closing the iron lid of the box. The twig seemed a token of great things to come.

"Suppose," he muttered softly, "she gave me a good horse. Wouldn't Dad be happy?"

He hurried to the hut and saw his mother seated by the table, both hands cupping her chin. The green and white kerchief she wore on her head slipped down her neck. Her eyes were swollen and her mouth was shaking. Peter's early return didn't startle her.

"Queen of heaven," she cried when she saw her son, "what a calamity! So many dues in arrears, and the tax people are taking all the hay, lad! What will the cattle live on through the winter, I ask you? But they wouldn't listen! They beat your poor dad with a stick, and I could not stand it, I just ran away. Is it his fault that the bees have failed and the hens have died? They say 'you have been gorging on honey and chickens, you lazy beggars!' Ah dear, those devils have brought so many papers with them. What can our folk make of those papers?"

Peter's shoulders shook.

"Oh, Mum, surely, not all the hay—"

"Every wisp of it," Marfa replied, "and old Michael's cow, too, and his wife—a sick woman! Nothing but milk to keep her going! And Semen's new harrow, and his old one is falling to pieces! Truly, son, those people are devils, and who is going to help us?"

"There is the Tsarina," Peter offered lamely, and Marfa's mouth tautened in a bitter line.

"Heavens, son, the Tsarina has never heard about us. What would it matter to her if all our cattle died in the winter? I reckon she would not notice if she lost a thousand cows. Oh dear, dear." She pushed a strand of mouse-colored hair off her forehead and added, "You're back early, son, and where are the raspberries?"

Peter blushed furiously.

"I came on a bear in Makar's Wood, Mum—that wild he looked—it was either the berries or me. But I'll make you fine new baskets, I promise."

Marfa sighed.

"Ah well, never mind! It's just one thing after another! What a calamity of a day—"

Peter got no beating. He moved away from the table and sat down by the opened door. The turmoil in the village rose to a deafening pitch. And then suddenly all was still. Marfa stirred.

"I reckon they have gone," she said thickly, "and may ten plagues run after them! I must go and see if poor old Michael has a drop of milk in the house. I might spare him a jugful—" She moved slowly, her shoulders bent, and a great wave of tenderness welled up in Peter's heart.

"Oh, Mum," he said huskily, "I wish I could do something—"

Marfa tried to smile at him.

"But you are a good lad," she said and went.

Presently she returned, and Zakhar came with her. Peter stifled a cry when he saw his father. There was dried blood across his right cheek. The gray smock was torn right across the shoulders, and red welts showed in between the rents. There seemed something dead in Zakhar's eyes. He bent his head under the lintel and almost tottered across to the trestle.

"Get me some water, wife," he said hoarsely. "Ah what a day! And those men call themselves christened folk, do they?" He stretched a shaking hand out for the crock and drank avidly. "Father Foma did what he could, God reward him, but did they listen? They said that we should have sent some paper or other about the bees and the hens. Whoever heard of such a thing? Did they expect the dead hens to tell them what they died of? And what a lot of arrears! As Semen said, the river might start running backward before we get clear of the debt. They say to me, 'One Vassilissa owes so many lengths of linen.' I say that Vassilissa has been dead these four summers. Do they believe me? Father Foma tells them he buried her. Do they believe him?"

"Mercy on us," said Marfa indignantly. "Old Vassilissa was never behindhand with a single tax. We all know it."

"So I said to one of them—'Will your honor have the coffin dug up and see if there is any linen buried with the bones?' He did not like me saying it." And Zakhara bent his huge matted head and took another drink of water.

"And what is going to happen now—"

"You will never guess, wife. Father Foma talked like the Christian he is, and the hay will remain, but there are so many other tangles that I, as the elder, must go to Moscow and see about them. Father Foma has grand friends there, and, wife, I think I will take the lad with me for company. Who knows—Moscow is such a holy city—there may well be some truly christened souls in those grand houses everybody talks about—"

"To Moscow?" Marfa echoed in horror. "Dad, that's the end of the world!"

"It is a good step," he agreed. "I reckon summer will be on the wane by the time we get back—"

"And you'll never find the way—" she stammered.

"I have a tongue in my head," said Zakhar. "Stands to reason that things should be settled—else those devils will leave us beggared for good. Well, lad." He turned to Peter. "You're coming along, do you hear?"

Peter did not answer. He could not tell if he were awake or dreaming.

3 Peter
makes a decision

hat bitterly turmoiled day came to its end, and the village was asleep. Peter had dragged his pallet near the door. He lay, staring at the deep blue cup of the sky studded with bright stars which, as he believed, were the souls of all the righteous folk turned to light in God's presence. It was a warm summer night, its stillness only occasionally broken by the footfall of an animal or the screech of an owl, a sharp, thin sword of a sound breaking from the neighboring wood.

Peter could not sleep. The morning's adventure in Makar's Wood now seemed dwarfed in his mind, conscious as he was of the stupendous journey to come. He could not even begin to imagine Moscow, its innumerable churches, its stone houses, and its crowds. For all he knew, the people of Moscow walked on golden pavements.

And yet his thoughts were not really engaged with the city he was going to see. The invasion of the tax collectors, their manhandling of his father, his mother's anguish—all he had seen and heard during the day ended by shaping a decision in Peter's mind. He would take his copper piece with him and, once they were in Moscow, he would find some learned clerk and ask him to write a very important letter for him. And he felt certain that a letter sent to the Empress from Moscow would reach her wherever she lived.

His mother had told him that the Empress knew nothing whatever about them at Malinka. Well, said Peter to himself, tossing from one side to the other on his mat, she would soon know that there was one Peter, son of Zakhar Belov, who wanted a chance to be taught his letters.

That is it, thought Peter, those men in uniform take notice of Father Foma and the Deacon because they are clergy, and they are supposed to know their letters. If I, a peasant's son, could read and write, they would take notice. If I knew what there was in those papers, old Michael would have kept his beast and my poor dad would not have been beaten. It is because the likes of us know nothing and stand in the dark. . . . The Tsarina will understand. When I have learned my letters, I will get back home and help the village with the tax people . . .

He knew well that neither Father Foma nor the Deacon would approve of his plan and he was determined to keep it a secret from everybody, Zakhar included. Peter fervently hoped that his copper piece would be enough to pay for the writing of the letter.

"It must be," he assured himself. "It feels so heavy"—and at last he fell asleep, and he dreamed of Princess Elizabeth mounted on a splendid gray and presenting him with a big book bound in red leather and clasped with silver.

A pale gray dawn broke over Malinka. Cattle lowed, cocks crowed, geese cackled, women, blue-painted wooden yokes across their shoulders, made for the river bank to fetch water, and lilac-blue whorls of smoke began weaving their way out of one doorway after another. All the miseries notwithstanding, the day's business had to be tackled, but that morning nobody sang at his work. A little later, on their way to the fields, some dozen men halted outside Zakhar's hut. Their eyes looked somber and their voices rang husky.

"You off today or tomorrow, Zakhar?" they wanted to know.

"In two days, neighbors. There is a tidy bit to get done—what with smocks and breeches to mend and wash and all—"

"Taking the lad with you, are you?"

"Yes, just for company."

"And you will tell them the truth," said a giant of a man with a bushy red beard and dark blue eyes. "Tell those grand folks that we are being fleeced right and left."

Here an old bent-shouldered man muttered into his matted gray beard:

"Zakhar, you tell them that we have scythes and hatchets, too, and that the river is near, and those devils with their papers might yet make a good dinner for our pike. Tell them that our patience is like a cracked crock already—it would not take much to smash it to pieces, Zakhar—"

Peter's father merely nodded.

Someone asked if he was likely to meet the Empress in Moscow.

"And what would she want with a poor peasant, neighbor?" protested Zakhar. "I reckon I might just as well meet Michael the archangel—"

"Well said," someone shouted, "and you would get more out of him than out of her—"

The mere sight of the tax collectors' green uniforms and brass buttons cowed the peasants. The day before they had not dared to give free rein to their feelings, but now they were again by themselves, no government spy lurking behind a tree to hear them and twist their words, and they felt they had earned the right to voice their indignation.

More and more men joined the little crowd, and mutterings ended in shouts. They had had more than enough, they told their obviously embarrassed elder, they were ready to go and tell their story in Moscow, they would walk all the way barefoot, tattered smocks on their shoulders. And they would not clamor for much—just their corn, their hay, their cattle . . .

And, whilst Zakhar stood silent, a man with a wart on his left cheek shouted over the others:

"Why go to Moscow, neighbors? Pokrovo Manor is a day's tramp from us. Let us go to her, Tsar Peter's daughter, and ask her to defend us. She is true. She is a Russian christened soul, and she likes all the common folk, too!"

"Yes, yes," shouted that oddly assembled parliament. "Let's make for Pokrovo—Princess Elizabeth will hear us all right."

Zakhar's blood all but froze in his veins. Here was high treason indeed! Even to name the young princess in private was not very safe in those days. To shout about her in a village street—Zakhar dared not think about it. He cleared his throat once or twice.

"Now, Christ save you, neighbors—" He leaned forward, arms akimbo, when he was interrupted by his own son's shrill voice shouting just behind him:

"They are right, Dad. Princess Elizabeth will listen to us. She is good. She likes common folk—"

"Well, said, lad," roared the whole assembly and, quick as lightning, Zakhar swung round and cuffed Peter hard.

"You—wooden-headed puppy," he thundered, "don't you know you might end on the gallows for such words?"

"But—" began Peter, and Zakhar would have hit him again if he had not ducked and run behind a high paling and vanished toward the fields, the crowd still clapping wildly. All prudence thrown to the winds, they shouted that the government would not have enough timber for all the gallows because everybody longed to see Princess Elizabeth on her father's throne. The tumult came to such a pitch that Zakhar began wondering if its echoes would travel far and wide and reach the neighboring villages in the end.

"Brothers, neighbors." He exerted his lungpower to the utmost. "Let us get back to the field work and forget this madness—"

"It is good sense," they shouted, when the thin, bent-shouldered figure of Father Foma appeared at the end of the street. The shabby brown cassock beating about his legs, the priest ran toward them, the summer wind tossing his long iron-gray locks.

They saw him, and at once the deafening shouts became sullen muttering.

Father Foma had been at Malinka for fifty years. He was neither good teacher nor preacher. He was not particularly brave or deeply spiritual. But he shared all their hardships and their poverty to the full. Through all the lean years his larder would be as bare as their own. He ministered to them as well as he could, and he did not refuse his services even when the people could not afford to give him a couple of eggs or a small rye loaf for a prayer or a requiem.

Now he stood among them, one bony hand playing with the untidy gray beard, his deep-sunken eyes sad rather than angry.

"It is a mutiny, Father Foma," muttered Zakhar, "that is what it is. God help me, I can do nothing. Sort it out, I beg of you—"

But the priest made no comment. His eyes swept over the crowd. He did not raise his voice when he said:

"Christ follow you all to the fields. Work waits for no man." Then he looked at Zakhar and added: "You and your son had better come to the church after vespers tomorrow, and I will sing a blessing for your journey."

"Thank you, Father Foma." Zakhar bowed from the hips. "Now might I just ask your reverence—"

But the priest waved his left arm and turned away. A silence stole upon the crowd. Heads bent, they dispersed.

Zakhar watched them go and he sighed. He felt with them and for them, but what could poor folk do against authority? He remembered a stray peddler telling him about numberless hangings and worse up and down the country.

"They strung up four men just for saying it was a shame *she* had not got a silver spoon to her name . . ."

And now, Zakhar thought unhappily, there was his own son joining in that madness. What did the lad know about *her*, Zakhar asked himself. He had better go, find Peter, and give him a good leathering. But Zakhar did not move.

"He is much too young . . . If I were to beat him hard, he might think there was something in it all," he thought, unaware of contradicting himself, because he knew only too well how much there was "in it all." "I'd best forget all about it. Father Foma says little enough, but he will keep order while I am away."

Meanwhile Peter, the hard cuff rubbed out of his memory, was in the beanfields, helping Mashka to fill the baskets she had brought.

Mashka, far too small for her ten years, always moved Peter to inarticulate pity. She was made up of all sorts of fears. She feared darkness and moonlight, spiders and frogs, owls and hares. It was something of a trial for Peter to take her for a walk in the woods, but things were certainly different in a beanfield, sunlight all over them and not a single hare in sight.

"Dad says you are going far, far away—" she offered shyly, her tiny freckled face turned away from him.

Peter nodded importantly.

"But I'll soon get back, Mashka—"

"I'm glad you have come out this morning. I have brought something." She stopped to rummage in a basket and produced a rather crumbly cabbage pie. "It might do for your dinner," she hurried on, her underlip trembling. "They have taken Dad's new harrow away, and Mum cried and cried. It was a good harrow, Peter."

"I shall try and bring it back, Mashka," Peter said recklessly, "and I'll try for a new scythe, too—"

Mashka's mouth stopped shaking, and her eyes, the color of cornflowers, flew wide in admiration. She would not have doubted Peter if he had said he would bring her a slice of the moon.

"All for my dad?—" she whispered.

"All for your dad," Peter affirmed, "and I shall bring you a scarlet kerchief and blue beads to wear to church—"

"But Mum would like the beads." Mashka paused, sucked her thumb for a moment, and added almost under her breath, "You have always been good to me."

"Take the beans home," Peter ordered and ran away.

He ran because he knew he had jobs to do that morning. Just beyond the beanfield he came on

29

Zakhar cutting the stubble for the winter fodder. Zakhar looked up, straightened his back, and thrust a sickle-shaped knife into Peter's hands.

"You should have started after breakfast," he said sternly. "Get on with the job. Mind, cut it close to the ground."

"Yes, Dad—"

Zakhar watched his son for a moment and then said:

"We are to have Father Foma sing a blessing for the journey."

"Yes, Dad. That will be good."

Zakhar scowled.

"I hope the blessing will drive all the nonsense out of your head."

Peter, his tousled fair head bent over the stubble, made no reply.

"And if you don't keep your mouth shut on the journey and in Moscow," Zakhar went on, "I will leather you good and hard. Now get on with the job—" He turned and stumped away toward the village where he told his wife that, though she had given him a fool of a son, Peter was not such a bad lad after all.

"Peter is no fool," cried Marfa indignantly, and Zakhar grinned.

"Well, wife, there are fools and fools in the world, and some are good enough for company."

"Peter is no fool," she repeated.

"Am I not taking him to Moscow?" asked Zakhar.

4 Peter's
letter is written

Zakhar and Peter left Malinka before dawn, the single little bell of the church jangling its Godspeed to them. The whole community, led by Father Foma and the Deacon, bore them company to the boundary of the parish. All walked in silence under a pale gray sky scumbled with uncertain blue here and there. Father and son were barefoot. They wore clean white smocks and linen breeches, their satchels strapped to their backs. They carried a little food, and Zakhar's satchel also had a box of flints and the papers entrusted to him by Father Foma.

At the farthest edge of the last field everybody stopped.

"Christ go with you," said Father Foma, and all the others echoed him. Marfa tried to keep back her tears, but they got the better of her. Trembling and crying, she embraced both husband and son, and then turned away, the wind playing with the ends of her green kerchief. The others stood still and silent. Zakhar and Peter moved on, neither turning his head.

All that day they walked along the river bank. The reach of the river so familiar to Peter was soon left behind. Beyond, the river widened, and there came twists and turns he had never seen. Sometimes their way led through fields sloping right down to the water. Sometimes they had to make their way through a tangled mass of undergrowth. At one point they reached a magnificent wood of silver birch and lime. Peter took off his smock and filled it with mushrooms.

It grew hot, and they did not hurry. Nor did they talk much. Toward evening they came to a sheltered spot fringed by thick clumps of wild honeysuckle and weeping willows. Peter at once gathered kindling for a fire. Zakhar got out his rod and cast off. He caught a big flat fish, and they supped off mushrooms and fish broiled in the ashes of the fire.

That proved to be the only night they spent in the open and the only occasion when they had to fall back on their own resources. At every village and hamlet reached at sundown, they would stop. Zakhar would give his name, mention his business, and offer his services, and everyone welcomed them as though they were friends. Zakhar and Peter earned shelter and food by mending a broken wheel here or a spike of a harrow there. Once Peter plaited a small basket for a housewife's little daughter. Her pleasure reminded him of Mashka, and he cried a little that night.

He had never imagined the journey would be so long, and sometimes he forgot all about Moscow. He felt lost in the immensity of space. Field, meadows, heath, and wood—it looked as if these would go on till the very end of the world. Once, through a sudden break in a wood Peter caught a glimpse of a big house in the distance. He gasped.

"Dad, is it Moscow then?"

"Bless you, lad!" Zakhar laughed. "How could it be?" And he peered hard. "It must be the home of some grand noble or other—"

"But it looks far bigger than all the huts at Malinka together—"

"I have heard it said that nobles live in such houses. Yes, it is big, but wait till you come to Moscow, son."

Yet Peter did not gasp when at last they reached the ancient city of seven hills. He was just dumb. And his eyes hurt him—there was so much to stare at. He clutched Zakhar's hand tighter and tighter because he was frightened of all those houses, church domes and cupolas, horses, carriages, people. Wave upon wave of sound, color, and movement all but engulfed Peter, and he wished he were a small boy again running to hide his face in his mother's comfortable lap. Zakhar glanced down at him.

"Tired, lad?" he muttered. "Bear up, though, we are nearly there—"

But they were not. Zakhar had been given full instructions by Father Foma how to find the street and the house of Master Ilya, parish clerk of St. Zossima's, whose wife, Matriona, was first cousin to Father Foma's wife. But the priest at Malinka had never been to Moscow, and the directions given by him were so fantastic that Zakhar soon knew they had lost their way. They wandered up and down several streets, and everywhere people seemed in such a hurry and were so well dressed that Zakhar did not dare to stop them and ask the way. At last, he stopped at a corner of a huge square, and a passing apple woman proved kindly and helpful.

"Bless you! St. Zossima's parish clerk—that would be Master Ilya. Indeed, I know him. You just turn here"—she pointed with a small bony hand—"and take the first turning left once you have passed Kalin's, the mercer, and go down the street, and there you are. It is the house with a blue pigeon painted over the door."

The way proved a bit longer than Zakhar thought. The sun was almost setting when they halted by the door with the blue pigeon, and Peter was so spent that he wished he might sprawl down on the cobbles and fall asleep, but he breathed more easily when the door was opened.

Master Ilya was a tall elderly man—with the chubbiest, kindliest face imaginable. He saw two dusty rather bedraggled peasants. They were strangers to him, and he had not been told about

34

their arrival, but he stood there smiling as though they had brought him a fine birthday present. When Zakhar, having first bowed from the hips two or three times, mumbled that they had come from Father Foma at Malinka, Master Ilya beamed at him.

"Never Father Foma of Malinka?" He opened the door wider. "Why, friends, the wife and his good woman were blood relations! Step in, step in! Walked all the long way, have you, by the looks of you? It is bed for you both once we have fed you, and the wife is just getting the supper ready. Step in, I say, and what business you have can wait till tomorrow—"

Zakhar mumbled that they had a little food of their own, they did not wish to give trouble, and a corner in the stable would do for them. . . .

Master Ilya would have none of it. And somehow or other Zakhar and Peter found themselves across the threshold and heard the host say that they were welcome guests and there was ample room in the house. A corner in the stable and their own provisions? Were they taking him, Master Ilya, for an infidel to let them sup off a crust when there was good cabbage soup and a meat pasty to follow?

Once inside, Peter stared about, bewilderment numbing all his senses. He could never have imagined a room like that—with three glazed windows, a wooden floor, a table covered with a fine white cloth, and chairs about. Master Ilya went on talking and Zakhar, bowing at every question, answered him, but Peter did not hear them. He just stared and stared, and wondered if he were awake or asleep. Then Matriona, small and plump, with a dimpled face and a smile as generous as her husband's, bustled in. Peter could not understand what she was saying, but her smile seemed reassuring. Somehow or other, he found himself in another room, standing by a table with a big basin full of water and a snow-white towel folded beside it. Matriona vanished to reappear with two white shirts, their collars embroidered in red.

Refreshed, and cool linen pleasant against the skin, Zakhar and Peter were called to take their places at the table in the main room. Hot soup steamed in large wooden bowls, and Peter knew he was famished. He dipped in his spoon and smiled shyly at his hostess. Never in all his life had he tasted such food.

When supper was over, Peter confronted yet another marvel: a room with two trestle beds in it, and each bed had a pillow and an embroidered blue coverlet.

"This will be something to tell the folk at home," said Zakhar.

Peter said nothing. He just tumbled down on the bed, laid one cheek against the pillow, and was fast asleep within an instant.

It was all like fairyland, and it continued day by day. Peter lived in a house, had three meals a day, and slept on a bed. Sometimes, his thin fingers clutching hard at Zakhar's big hairy hand, he ventured out into that frightening, exciting, incredible world where so many people moved about as though they had nothing to do but walk up one street and down another. Little by little, Peter's initial fear and bewilderment ebbed away; he began making comparisons between life in Moscow and in the countryside, and he said to himself that all the marvels in the city could not make up for the lack of air and space.

Meanwhile Master Ilya had looked through all the papers sent by Father Foma.

"You are certainly in a sad muddle down at Malinka," he said to Zakhar, "but God is merciful." And he started shepherding Zakhar from one office to another. One evening, when they were alone in their room, Peter dared greatly and asked his father how the business was getting on.

"It will soon be straightened out, so Master Ilya says, but I can't tell anything, lad. They have got their noses buried in their papers, and not a man do I meet but his one quill in his hand and another stuck behind his ear. I wonder that there are any geese left in the country—here, they use quills by the hundred."

"Dad, have you told them about Semen's harrow and all?"

Having asked, Peter bit his lip furiously as he remembered the foolish promise he had given to Mashka. Bring her beads and kerchiefs from Moscow? How could he? The city was full of shops, but you did not get a string of beads for a dozen eggs: you had to pay money for everything.

"Indeed, I have," Zakhar replied, "and they wrote it all down and read it out to me, and now Master Ilya says they are writing more papers about it."

It all sounded extremely complicated. Peter asked no more questions. His own problem was troubling him. The letter to the Tsarina must be written, but by whom? He dared not approach any stranger. There was Master Ilya, whose kindness remained the same, but Peter had not the temerity to ask him.

"It will have to be that scribe," he decided, "but will he keep my secret?"

Every morning a thin, bent-shouldered man came into the house. His clothes were shabby and put on anyhow. He shuffled rather than walked. He kept his head down and spoke to nobody. He worked in a slip of a room at the back, and shared their dinner. If Master Ilya or Matriona asked him a question, he answered briefly, but so hungry did he look that Peter hoped a copper piece might tempt the man.

One morning, the coin held tight in his hand, Peter opened the door of the little room. His disheveled head on the table, Egor the scribe was fast asleep. The creak of the door startled him, and his red-lidded eyes peered at Peter.

"Yes, boy?" he asked none too amiably.

Peter walked up to the table and laid the copper coin in front of Egor, who leaned back in his chair and stared hard.

"What's that?"

"It is for you, Master," Peter said shyly. "Could you write a letter for me, please?"

Egor's thin face puckered up in a grin.

"To your girl in the country, I suppose? But you look a bit young to me, lad—"

"No, Master. To the Tsarina wherever she lives," Peter said quietly.

The scribe stared harder than ever. A mouse

scuttled across the floorboards. In the silence that followed Peter could almost hear his own heart beating.

"Say it again," Egor said thickly.

"To the Tsarina wherever she lives," the boy repeated. "You will know where that is, Master. I don't."

"What do you wish to say to her?" asked Egor.

Peter swallowed hard. It had been such a cherished secret of his. It seemed almost impossible to find words for it.

"Well?" the scribe prompted him.

"That I would like to learn my letters," Peter blurted out.

Egor did not reply in a hurry. He scratched his head. He rubbed his nose. He stroked his chin. Then he looked at Peter so piercingly that the boy was more scared than ever. Yet it was too late to turn back.

"And why do you wish to learn your letters?" Egor asked at last.

Peter looked at his bare roughened feet, cleared his throat, and began lamely:

"Well, Master, there is so much to put right what with the hay and all—and I thought I might help my dad if I could read and write—it's hard for him often enough—seeing he doesn't know what there is in all the papers—and there are all the other folks, too—see, Master . . . Back at home, Father Foma is always busy . . . I once asked the Deacon and he said books were not for the likes of me, seeing I was a peasant's son—but I think the Deacon was wrong—" And, having delivered the longest speech in his life, Peter drew a much-needed breath and kept his eyes bent for fear of what he might see in Egor's face.

There followed a very brief pause. Then the scribe spoke quietly:

"Lad, it is the finest job I have ever had given me . . . Come here tomorrow, and you shall have your letter, and I know an honest man or two who will see to it that it reaches the Tsarina. But you must promise me by the cross you wear that you will not tell a living soul that I wrote a letter for you. In my turn I shall keep the bargain. Let it be a secret between us."

"Yes, Master." And Peter pulled out his tiny baptismal cross from under his smock and kissed it in token of his promise.

Egor had the letter ready the next morning. It was written on a large sheet of wonderful thick paper, and Peter gasped when he saw the beautifully written lines.

"Now listen when I read it to you," said Egor, "and then you must put your mark at the foot of the sheet—just a cross, see—" And he cleared his throat and began:

"Most gracious Sovereign and Empress, prostrate at the august feet of your Imperial Majesty, I, Peter, son of Zakhar Belov, the elder of the village of Malinka near the town of Kaluga, a serf of the Crown and the least worthy of all the slaves of your Imperial Majesty, hereby make my most humble petition to the august ears: graciously to bestow on my unworthiness the precious favor of learning my letters to the end that I may serve your Imperial

Majesty in a manner most pleasing to my august Sovereign, whose profitable servant I remain unto my death. And in witness whereof I venture to append the mark of the cross made by my own hand and, prostrate at the august feet, implore your Imperial Majesty to have mercy upon my temerity."

Peter heard it all, his mouth wide open, his eyes big with wonder. The sonorous words meant nothing to him. When Egor laid down the great sheet, he stammered:

"It—is—very fine, Master—there is far too much for one copper piece—but—there is nothing of what I told you—"

"There is everything," Egor broke in, not unkindly. "See, lad, I had to word it all differently; I could not use the words you gave me. The Tsarina is not a peasant woman. Now you mentioned hay to me, didn't you? Well, for all I know she has never seen an armful of hay in her life. Now you just put the cross down here—and I will see to the rest."

When it was done, Egor looked at Peter and said almost sharply:

"And mind you remember your promise, lad. Not a word to anyone here in Moscow—not even to your dad, at least not for a time. And I wish you all the luck in the world!"

Peter thanked him and ran away. He felt at once happy and frightened, but he knew that he could trust that thin, tattered man. And Peter was not mistaken: Egor would keep his promise.

Soon after, the Malinka business was settled by

the gentlemen with quills stuck behind their right ear, and Master Ilya explained to Zakhar that all the arrears were remitted to the little community. There followed a generous Godspeed from the host and hostess, and Zakhar and Peter got ready for their journey home.

"At least the cattle won't go hungry in the winter, Christ reward Master Ilya," said Zakhar to his son.

Peter indeed felt happy about the outcome, but all his thoughts were worlds away from the village matters. He wondered about the letter now sure to be on its way to the capital. He supposed that Father Foma would read the Tsarina's reply to him, and he decided to tell his father nothing until that reply came to Malinka.

5 What
happened to Peter's
letter

nd now they were in winter. All the excitements of the summer seemed as though they had never been. Malinka settled down to the pattern known to its forefathers for centuries, with the hens and the geese brought into the huts full of acrid smoke all day and all night, the cattle and what very few horses there were all housed in stable and byre, the women cooking, spinning, and weaving all day long, and those men who were lucky enough to possess stout boots and sheepskins venturing out in the blizzards and snowdrifts to trap a hare and so relieve the monotony of salt fish, gruel, and pickled cabbage.

And Peter waited. He had been kept busy enough all through the autumn helping his parents to sort out the root vegetables, to store the corn ground at the monastery mill down the river, to string dried onions and mushrooms together and hang them down from the ceiling, and to chop endless cabbage heads for his mother to pickle. All those were familiar tasks, and his mind was always occupied with his secret. He knew he could not expect any answer to his letter until the spring, and at times it was hard to wait so long.

He had had one sharply awkward moment on his return from Moscow, with Mashka expecting her red kerchief and the beads. He had tried to explain that things were quite different in the city.

"You need coins for everything you want to have—"

The cornflower eyes, brimming with tears, had then stared at him.

"What is a coin?"

"Why, money," and Peter had tried to make it clear, but Mashka had wept and wept.

"Wait till the spring," he had promised rather lamely.

One evening, the frugal supper eaten, Marfa sat spinning by firelight, and Peter crouched on the earthen floor. From the top of the stove came Zakhar's measured snoring, and suddenly Peter grew very bold.

"Mum," he said in a whisper, "so many people did I see in Moscow, and nobody at all mentioned Princess Elizabeth."

Marfa, her foot on the treadle, threw a frightened glance at him.

"It is better so, lad. Dad always says so, and he should know."

Peter nodded and did not reply. For one wild moment he wished he might tell his mother his secret.

But he said nothing. Next morning he worked his way through the deep snow at the back of the hut and got into the tumbledown shed. He could not dislodge the soil in the farthest corner—it was frozen stiff. But he stooped and thought about his twig of the crimson oak and of the lady with dark blue eyes and a mischievous smile. It was somehow good to think of her—as good as eating hot gruel on a cold morning.

However slow was the pace of the long wintry months, spring came at last, and Malinka stirred into heightened activity, but no reply came to Peter's letter. His patience strained to the utmost, he still waited, and never for a moment did he think that Egor had failed him.

They were at the height of summer. It was the eve of Trinity Sunday, and all the morning Peter was busily cutting big branches of birch to decorate the church and the village for the festival. Very thirsty, his face beaded with sweat, he was making for home when Zakhar met him at the edge of the little spinney. Zakhar's weatherbeaten face reflected such horror that Peter halted, his hands shaking.

"Dad, Dad." He moistened his lips. "Why? What's happened?"

Zakhar wiped his forehead with a great hairy hand.

"I wish I knew." He spoke like a man pushed to the edge of a precipice. "But they won't tell me . . .

45

They won't let me be there, even . . . Whatever have you done, lad? Now run home—your mother's looking for a clean shirt for you—and then make for Father Foma's. They are there."

"Who, Dad?"

But Zakhar shook his head and turned away.

Peter ran. In the hut Marfa was weeping, but she knew no more than her husband did. She found a clean smock for Peter, and then thrust an iron-framed icon of Our Lady into his hands.

"See, son," she gulped and stopped to wipe her tears, "that's my mother's blessing. The frame opens at the back. Put a little blessed soil from the churchyard into it. That will protect you—"

Suddenly she flung both arms around Peter's neck and held him so hard that for a second he could hardly breathe.

"Son, little son," she muttered, "when you were up there in Moscow, meeting all manner of folk, you never mentioned that lady to anyone, did you?"

"Never, Mum," he answered brokenly, rubbed his face against her wet cheek, and ran to the back of the hut straight into the shed. Whatever was to happen, he must not lose his precious little twig. He thrust it inside the iron frame, slipped the thin chain over his neck, and raced toward Father Foma's house.

People were standing at every doorway, but none spoke to Peter, nor would he stop to look at anyone. He did not know about the blow fallen on Malinka: away in the spinney, Peter had not heard the dread slogan of the Secret Chancery, "Deed and Word," thundered down the village street. He had

46

not seen the three men in green uniform ride past the humped little church. They had summoned Peter, Zakhar Belov's son, and the summons, explaining nothing to the peasant mind, had cloaked the whole village with terror.

In the priest's living room, three middle-aged men, bewigged and green-coated, sprawled on a settle behind a table littered with papers. Pale and trembling, Father Foma stood in a corner, his left hand clutching at his cross. The newcomers took as much notice of him as though he were a fly on the wall, but his was the only dwelling in the village they cared to enter.

The men's clean-shaven faces looked hard and slightly bored. The fat man in the middle fingered a paper, then re-lit his pipe, and drummed his fingers on the table.

"What a nuisance," he said to the other two, "and to think we have to stop at four more places between here and Kaluga. What is the country coming to? It is six of them we have to take to Moscow, isn't it?"

The others nodded. Father Foma's hands were shaking. He recognized the alien accent: the three men were Germans . . .

Peter ran in and halted at the door. The priest dared not look at him. The fat man knit his bushy eyebrows and said thickly:

"Come nearer! And answer all the questions unless you want a flogging!"

The man on his left grinned unpleasantly:

"Ah, he'll get one all right—"

The fat man stared hard at Peter and raised a big sheet of gray paper.

"Is that your mark at the bottom?"

Peter's heart thudded: it was his letter to the Tsarina. What were those angry men doing with it? The gray paper looked so dirty and the upper left-hand corner was torn off. Did the Tsarina not wish to answer it at all? But he had meant no harm . . . He moistened his lips.

"Answer the question," shouted the fat man.

"Yes, Master."

"Did your father know about it?"

"No, Master."

"Who wrote it for you?"

"A clerk, Master—when my dad and I were in Moscow—" Peter's voice rang a little more steady.

"His name?"

"I can't call it to mind, Master."

"So you want your memory refreshed, do you?"

The officer half-rose from the trestle and struck Peter so hard that he tottered and fell on the floor. In his corner Father Foma closed his eyes. But he could not stop his ears. He heard the sickening impact of a second blow, a third, and a fourth. Not a sound came from Peter. The priest opened his eyes again and forced himself to look. Peter lay on the ground, his clean smock all but torn off his shoulders, blood streaming down his face and neck. And the priest, who had never been very brave in all his life, stepped away from the corner and raised a shaking hand.

"Let him stand his trial, Masters, but don't kill him—"

Two of the men scowled. The third spluttered angrily:

"Silence, Father. We have come on her Majesty's

business. Do you wish to be hanged for taking sides with a traitor?"

"The boy is no traitor—"

"He is guilty of a conspiracy against her Majesty's august person. He has dared to address a petition to her Majesty, he—a Crown serf, asking to be given a chance to learn his letters. It is all down here in black and white. The matter has been dealt with by the Secret Chancery in St. Petersburg: we carry General Oushakov's instructions, and our commission comes from his Highness the Duke. Whoever heard of a serf learning his letters? Of course he is a traitor, but he must have had accomplices—that clerk for one. We have had no instructions about his father, more is the pity." And the officer stretched out a booted leg and kicked Peter. "Now then, you—puppy—who wrote the letter for you?"

Peter slowly scrambled up to his feet. But he made the same reply through his swollen lips:

"I can't call it to mind—"

They struck him again and again until his whole body was a bruise and he could hardly make out the legs of the table for the blood running down from a gash on his forehead. Dumbly he felt as though he were being pushed down into a pit where no daylight was. But his lips were set and he made no reply. In the end he tottered down again and did not move.

"Tell the men to bring the carts along," the fat officer barked at one of his colleagues. "We must get to Kaluga before nightfall, and the roads here would put an angel out of temper."

Father Foma's face was ashen. He felt terribly

scared, but his high moment was there and he did not shirk it. He spoke fast and urgently:

"I've known the boy all his life. There is no harm in him. He is a good worker and intelligent. Whoever wrote that letter for him must have known he meant no harm. I have sometimes wondered if I should teach him myself, but what with the parish and all, there is no leisure left—"

"Ah," said the fat man, "here is a sermon in little! Why, we might level a charge against you! Teaching letters to a serf? What next?"

"Then take me," cried the priest. "Beat me, hang me, do what you like: I am old, my days are counted—but leave the child alone . . . Heaven knows a peasant's life is hard enough—"

The officer pursed his lips.

"What a pity you are a cleric—but your bishop shall hear of it. Ah, the carts are here!" He looked at Peter and shouted, "Up you get, puppy—"

Peter heard the order as though from a distance. He tried to scramble to his feet. After a second effort he shuddered, slumped down, and lay quite still. The fat man looked so furious that for an instant the priest thought he would see Peter killed under his roof. But the officers of the Secret Chancery had different instructions. Peter was dragged out, thrown into one of the carts, and the three men left the house without a single word to Father Foma.

At every doorway men, women, and children watched the carts go, frozen terror in their eyes. The people of Malinka were not really cowards, but they knew only too well that it was hopeless for them to interfere. When the clouds of gray-yellow dust had settled down, they began stirring out of their nightmare. An old woman crossed herself and mumbled:

"God give rest to the lad's soul. Now, neighbors, let us do honor to the parents."

They all turned indoors and looked for some scrap of white stuff to put on because white was the color of mourning. That done, all of them moved toward Father Foma's little house.

Tears trickling down his thin cheeks, the old man came out to them. They stood there asking no questions. For a few moments pastor and flock stood gazing as though the last shred of articulacy had left them. Then someone said tremulously:

"We'll all come to the requiem, Father Foma—"

"The lad was alive when they took him." The priest swallowed hard.

"What did they say he had done?" a woman ventured to ask.

"Treason?"

The word stirred them all.

"As well charge a grasshopper with treason—"

"Shall we ever see justice done?"

"Such a decent lad, too, never harmed anyone—"

Those were all sullen mutters, but the priest knew well that the low-keyed protests screened the rumbling menace of a storm. He thought swiftly: Yes, they would take their scythes and hatchets and try to avenge Peter, and what would come of it? They would all be hanged, and he raised his head and schooled himself to speak calmly:

"I mean to find it all out, neighbors. There is the

bishop, for one. Don't despair—there is justice with God, and now I must go and see Zakhar." He came down the steps and the crowd sighed as they watched him go.

The door of Zakhar's little hut was shut tight. The priest had to knock twice before Peter's father appeared, deep winter in his eyes.

"The wife is asleep," he murmured. "So spent she was with her tears I made her lie down, but come in, Father Foma, come in. It is kind of you."

The priest stepped inside. Zakhar went on:

"There is the wife, see? I did not want her to be made a widow today—so I stayed with her—else I would have strangled those devils with my bare hands. Will they hang him in the end? And what do they say he has done?"

Very briefly the priest told Zakhar about the letter to the Tsarina. Peter's father clenched his fists.

"Will the sun ever rise over the land? To take a lad for a piece of foolishness! And he doesn't know his letters. How could he have written it?"

"Someone in Moscow wrote it for him, Zakhar—"

"When I was in the city," Zakhar whispered hoarsely, "Master Ilya told me about Tsar Peter. *He* would have clapped the lad on the shoulder. But things are different now. Serfs we are, and serfs are like worms—"

"Zakhar—"

"No, Father Foma, it is time I spoke out. God made the four seasons, but it looks as though winter alone were meant for us peasant folk. . . . Ah, lad, had you but told me . . . Is there anyone to see that some justice is done to him?"

"I shall write to Master Ilya at the first opportunity, Zakhar. He is a great man in Moscow—he will do his best—"

"I wish we had never gone there." Zakhar bent his head. "I did put a thing or two right for the neighbors but what is it when you think of this mischief?"

For a moment Father Foma stood silent. Then he raised his head and such a light flashed into his eyes that anyone except Zakhar might have wondered if the priest were standing on top of a hill at dawn, his face turned to the east.

"Zakhar," he said slowly, "there will be anxiety and much hard waiting ahead, but all shall end in God's mercy, I know—"

Peter's father did not reply. The priest turned and left him.

6 At the sign of the blue pigeon

It was autumn. After a fortnight of bitterly cold rain, Moscow was wrapped in a thick fog for several days. When it cleared, the waters of the Moskva and the Yauza were running sluggishly, a thin grayish film covering them. The skies looked as though they were cut out of thick gray cloth. It was bitterly cold, but there was no wind, and people said to one another that the air had gone to prison. At the Gostiny Dvor mercers and other shopkeepers wondered if they had better put up their shutters, so few were their customers. It was not the kind of weather to lure many people out of doors.

About noon the urgent haste of hoofs was heard in the distance. A crown courier, his buff and red uniform muddied and dusty, was soon galloping furiously toward one of the gates of the Kremlin, and here and there anxious voices were raised:

"A courier—from the capital?"

"So there is news—"

"Are we at war?"

The day's lethargy vanished like smoke. Crowds, nobody answering their questions, began converging toward the Kremlin. Suddenly a great bell began tolling from one of the Kremlin's belfries. At once everybody's eyes were strained toward the rampart a little to the left of the Spassky Gate where an official appeared, a paper fluttering in his hands. The tolling ceased. Into the stillness came the deafening voice of the city crier:

"Orthodox people, pray for the soul of our right sovereign lady the Empress Anna." He paused and went on, his considerable lung power strained to the utmost—"Long live our soverign lord the Emperor Ivan VI!"

It was comparatively safe to be astonished at the name of her successor. He was Anna's great-nephew, some said, born that very summer, wasn't he? A five-month-old infant to be their sovereign lord? It made no sense to them. Who could crown a baby in his cradle?

They did not weep for Anna. They did not cheer Ivan VI. They dispersed to their homes and remembered their dinner.

A week or so later, in a narrow street beyond the Arbat Square, in a house with a blue pigeon painted over the door, Master Ilya, the parish clerk of St. Zossima's, and Egor, his scribe, sat facing each other in a small room at the back of the kitchen. Neither man seemed at ease.

"See if there is anyone listening by the yard door," muttered Master Ilya, and Egor assured him that there was not a soul.

"Forty-six years old the Tsarina, and now gone to her judgment, and a hard judgment it is sure to be, heaven forgive me," said Master Ilya, "but what is to happen now, Egor? An infant for a Tsar and a German at that! And who is to rule in his name? A pack of German fortune-hunters? And for how many years?"

Egor's disheveled head was bent low.

"I have heard folk say that the child's mother has about as much sense as a plucked hen. It is nothing but clothes and dancing with her! Ah me, no daylight to be seen for the country!"

At these words the scribe raised his head.

"Isn't there, Master Ilya?" he challenged. "And what of the North Star?"

"Sh-sh." Master Ilya raised both hands in horror. "Do you want the Secret Chancery people to swoop down on us? Mark my words, Egor, they will be busier than ever now."

"I didn't name her, did I? I didn't say 'Princess Elizabeth,' did I? But I shall, from now on—"

"Egor, Egor, for mercy's sake? . . ."

"Well, Master Ilya, you think the same as I do. It is for Tsar Peter's daughter to rule over us, and where is she?"

"Recalled from her exile, so I hear," Master Ilya murmured, his eyes rather anxiously scanning the little yard outside the window. "She still has a palace of her own in St. Petersburg. I reckon those Germans think it safer to have her under their eye than out in the country."

"They will try and poison her—" Egor said almost under his breath.

"God will preserve her," Master Ilya said heavily, "and now we had better do some work, Egor—"

"The new prison in the parish, you mean?"

"Yes . . . it looks as though every parish in Moscow will soon have a prison of its own. Fancy taking those wine vaults of Tarassov's! Not enough prison space for all the criminals, they say, but there is no increase in real crime—so far as I can see. Roads are unsafe, but we have always had highwaymen, haven't we? And it is not brigands they are after either! It is always treason, treason, treason." He sighed and picked up a sheaf of papers. "We'd better have a look at the list of those about to be transferred to Tarassov's, and I should say most of them are as guilty as a babe unborn—" Master Ilya put his iron-rimmed spectacles on his nose and started reading. In a moment he dropped the paper and stared at Egor.

"What was the name of that village elder we had with us just over a year ago, wasn't it? He came from Father Foma, kinsman of my wife. The man had such a bright lad with him, too—"

"Why," Egor replied, "Zakhar Belov. He came with papers about tax remissions, from Malinka near Kaluga."

"So it was! You have a jewel of a memory, Egor. Well, he is here—"

"Zakhar?"

57

"No, the lad—Peter, yes, here is the name, Peter Belov."

"No!" Egor jumped to his feet.

"Yes, first sent to Taganka Prison, now to be transferred to Tarassov's! Saints preserve us! To keep a child in a dungeon! A bad Easter to them all." Master Ilya got up. "Egor, you get on with the work. I must go to Taganka and find out what has happened. Such a bright lad he was, as much harm in him as in a fly!" As he made for the door, Egor said in a harsh voice:

"Master Ilya, it is for me to go there, not you—"

"What do you mean?"

Egor moistened his lips.

"Why, why," he faltered, "it may all be because of a letter I wrote for him."

"A letter? To whom?"

"The late Tsarina. . . . The lad thought he would be of more use to his community if he knew his letters. He could not stay here in Moscow and there was nobody to teach him in the country. It was a wonderful thought, Master Ilya, and I wrote it properly for him, with all the titles and everything, and he promised on the cross he would never tell anyone I had done it for him." Egor added: "He paid for it too—with a copper piece. I took it. I saw that he wanted me to have it."

Ilya stared at his scribe.

"There was nothing wrong in the letter? No complaints about taxes or anything like that?"

"Nothing except what I have told you."

Master Ilya started getting into his sheepskins.

"Whatever trouble the lad got himself in can have

58

nothing to do with the letter you wrote for him," he said hoarsely. "Stay here, Egor, and wait for me."

Left alone in the little room, the clerk hid his face in both hands. He had meant to help Peter. He kept remembering that candid face with its dark blue eyes, that shock of flaxen hair, that very earnest voice . . . And Egor had not forgotten his own words: "It's the finest job I have ever been given to do. . . ." So he had thought at the time. So he thought still. What did it matter, he thought furiously, if you were a peasant or a merchant, a priest or a soldier, a noble even? Enlightenment should be open to anyone who wanted it.

Daylight had gone. Almost unaware, the clerk got up, struck fire from the flint box, and lit the two tallow candles in wooden sticks. Then he sat still, staring at the blue-yellow flames, and he never knew how long he had sat, the work wholly forgotten.

The door creaked plaintively. Egor rose and raised a candlestick shoulder-high. It was Master Ilya, and his face looked gray.

"Well, Egor," he said with an effort to smile, "I may have put my own head into the noose, but I am past caring."

The clerk asked almost inaudibly:

"Was it because of that letter?"

"Yes." Master Ilya slumped down on the nearest chair. "The governor of Taganka was civil enough—for all he is a German. He let me see it. It is just as you said—there is not a wrong word in it, and they don't know that you wrote it."

"But they asked the lad surely—"

59

"Asked him? Man, they tried to beat it out of him, and he wouldn't tell them. There is a decent lad for you, and they have pushed him into a dungeon—"

"What is going to happen?"

"Well, it looks as though the Tsarina's death and all has put a spoke in their wheel. Some papers have got lost, for one thing. The governor said they were going to keep him until they had further instructions. It seems they got Peter and six other peasants into their net at the same time. Always the same charge—treason! They'll soon see treason in an overbaked loaf!"

Egor asked with difficulty:

"Master, have you seen Peter?"

"They would not let me. I told them I would stand surety for the lad. I said, 'Let me have him in my own house; if any harm come of it, let it be laid at my door. The wife and I are in the fullness of years,' I told them, and would they listen? Then I fear I let myself go a bit. I told the governor and two other bewigged scoundrels in the room that if Tsar Peter were alive he'd take his stick to them for foolishness, that he'd have been pleased to get a letter like that, that lads like Peter should be treasured like pearls and not treated as though they were of no account in the land. I should not have said such things, Egor. Now they won't transfer him to Tarassov's. They are keeping him where he is." Master Ilya drew a much-needed breath. "Why, where are you off to?" he cried on seeing Egor snatch at his fur cap and sheepskins and make for the door.

"You'll have to find another clerk, Master Ilya. My job is to go to Taganka and to tell the governor I wrote that letter. Let them hang me if they wish—but they must let the boy go—" and Egor was almost through the door when Master Ilya shouted:

"You stay where you are and that's an order—"

"And let the boy rot in prison?"

"Your giving yourself up won't give him freedom. Don't you know better than that? What's more, you can't control yourself when you are angry—you'll give them more than enough rope to hang you, and none of it will help the lad. They would think they had evidence enough of a conspiracy—and that will bring the boy to the gallows as sure as I am parish clerk of St. Zossima's," said Master Ilya weightily.

Egor stood hesitant.

"But I have brought him into it," he mumbled at last. "Is it right that I should be at liberty and—"

"Now, my friend," said Ilya persuasively, "I do understand what you feel, but stop thinking about yourself for a bit. The boy never betrayed you, all the more honor to him—"

"And so I must let him rot to death at Taganka?" Egor flung bitterly.

"And so you must be sensible. You owe it to him. God's justice is there—however screened it be from our eyes. Egor, say a prayer for the lad and come to supper, and mind not a word about him at the table. I don't want to upset the wife. I shall tell her presently, see?"

7 Peter
starts a new
life

Everything was not ended, thought Peter, because nobody had tried to take away the little iron-framed icon he wore on his breast. Now it was the only possession he had. His clothes were in tatters.

He could not remember much of the long journey from Malinka to Kaluga and then on to Moscow. Somewhere or other more prisoners joined him in the cart, but nobody spoke. He lay at the bottom of the cart, manacles on his hands and feet, and they were unnecessary since he could not have moved an inch, his body bruised and battered all over.

There were many halts on the way; long nights spent in cellars, hours of jolting along rough roads, crocks of tepid soup, hunks of stale bread, and water brought by strangers who could not speak without swearing. The cellars were dark and the hood drawn over the cart shut off what comfort might have been offered by a glimpse of the sky. But all of it together was tied into a knot in Peter's mind. All seemed remote and unreal. The little icon remained the only link between him and a way of life he could understand. Gradually, toward the end of the journey, separate details from the past became clear in Peter's thoughts—the dented cauldron at home, the satiny sheen of a cow's flank, a clump of wild marigolds at the edge of the oak spinney, the abrupt beat of a pike's tail, the sharp smell of rain-washed grass, the feel of soft mud between his bare toes, the measured whirr of his mother's spinning wheel. All of it came in shape, color and sound. Of his parents Peter dared not think at all.

Very gradually he began to wonder what it really was that they had accused him of. Was it possible that Egor had put something different into the letter? It could not be. That dreadful fat man in the priest's house had read the letter aloud to him. It had sounded exactly the same as what Egor had written.

At the thought of Egor, a strange warmth stole into the boy's mind: he had not broken his promise, he had not mentioned Egor's name.

At last, all movement came to an end. The hood was pulled off the cart, and a stranger in a smart blue coat came up and ordered the prisoners to get down. Someone's rough hands loosened Peter's chains for him. His bare feet on the cobbles, he looked about. They were in a great forecourt with high stone walls, pierced by small windows, on every side. There was a slit of a doorway just ahead. All of them stumbling, the prisoners made toward it. They were brought into a huge vaulted room. A bewigged man in a blue uniform, who looked as though he were made of leather and iron, sat behind a table. He took no notice of the new arrivals. An elderly clerk rummaged among some papers and called out in a thin screeching voice:

"Come forward, 259."

From the well of the room a woman in a faded crimson gown and a gray shawl tottered toward the table. The bewigged man did not look at her. He turned to the clerk:

"Has the case been settled?"

"Yes, your Honor." The clerk bowed so low that his head all but brushed against the edge of the table. "259 was settled just over a year ago, but some of the papers were lost. Here is the High Court's decision."

The bewigged man took the paper, glanced at it, and spoke in the same impersonal voice:

"259, you are charged that on 10th June 1737, in the presence of four witnesses, outside a fishmonger's shop in Tverskaya Street in the city of Moscow, you spat at the mention of the name of his Grace the Duke of Courland to the dishonor of our right sovereign lady the Empress and the Imperial family. Ten years of penal servitude are appointed to you, the sentence to begin from August 1738."

This time the woman did not totter. She sprang

forward, arms raised, "My children . . . My children . . . Have mercy . . . have mercy—" She fell and beat her head against the ground.

"Take her away," said the man at the table. "Clerk, call the next—"

Peter, shaking from head to foot, leaned against the wall and closed his eyes. Subdued sighing arose from the well of the room.

"Quiet," thundered the officer.

Peter, his eyes still closed, felt that he had fallen into a bottomless pit. Number after number was called by the clerk, there was much shuffling of feet, the cold measured voice of the officer, someone cried, someone else sighed. It was all part of a nightmare, he, Peter, could have no share in, and yet he was in it.

The clerk screeched:

"439, come forward—"

Nobody stirred. Peter opened his eyes. An armed guard came up to him and gave him a push.

"Come forward, you! That is your number—"

Peter never knew how he crossed the big room. His teeth were chattering.

"Inquiries about 439 and six others are not yet complete in St. Petersburg, your Honor," said the clerk with another deep bow.

"Dungeon 3 for 439," said the officer, when someone behind Peter moved a step forward.

"May it please your Honor, prisoner 439 is from the country—"

"I know that, and so are the other six. They have caused us enough trouble already fetching them. Well?"

"It is the victuals, your Honor—"

"Taganka is a prison and not an inn. He may get food if he is lucky. That is not our business. We may soon get instructions about him and those others. For all you know, they might not be here very long."

"Come along," said the guard to Peter.

It was difficult to walk and it proved a long way to go until they reached the top of a wide stairway leading downward. It was fitfully lit, the steps worn and slippery, but there was a rail of sorts, and Peter followed the man to the bottom. He heard the sharp impact of iron on iron, and a great door was flung open. The guard pushed Peter in, and in an instant the door swung to and the key was turned in the lock. He stood still, his head bent, and a silence welcomed him. Presently the sound of low-keyed voices reached him, and he raised his head.

He stood at one end of an enormous stoneflagged room. What light there was came through a few latticed apertures set almost flush with the ceiling. There did not seem to be any furniture. The air was so noisome that he found it hard to breathe. Bemused, he stood and stared at what appeared a crowd of men and women, some crouching on the floor, others leaning against walls. They were many, but to him they appeared as one pallid face and all their murmurs reached him as one voice.

"Saints defend us, why, it is a child!"

"Heaven have mercy on him!"

"Poor lad!"

"Look, look, neighbors, he is going to fall—"

There followed a rapid concerted movement toward Peter. Roughened hands caught at him and held him. Someone pressed a mug of water against his lips. A woman's voice rang close to his ear.

"Christ save you, child! Don't fret—we'll look after you."

That unexpected kindness proved too much. Peter, held in a stranger's arms, lost consciousness.

There were about fifty men and women in Dungeon 3, Taganka Prison, and they all belonged to Moscow. Not one of them had been put on trial. In most cases, some imprudent word, overheard by a Secret Chancery agent, had led to an instant arrest. Their names, listed in the prison records, were not used by the staff. They were just so many numbers and, as Peter was to learn, some among them had been there for years, others for a few months.

Neither the governor nor the members of his staff ever came to see them. Twice a day the great doors would be opened, and guards came in with water, logs for the huge stove, and whatever provisions had been left by prisoners' relatives and friends. Taganka provided a roof, water, and fuel—but no food.

On Saturday evenings, Sunday mornings, and on certain great feasts the doors would be flung open. A platoon of soldiers, armed with muskets, stood on guard, and the prisoners crowded near the doors. They could see the wide stairway running up and they could hear the chaplain and his deacon singing mass and vespers. There were no other ministrations afforded them, and before the last Amen reached them, the great doors were closed and barred again. There being no candles, the prisoners had to grope to their places along the dank stony walls.

They were never taken out for exercise. On rare occasions, one of the guards would call out a number, and the prisoner went never to return, and the rest could not tell if he or she went to the gallows or to freedom. Again occasionally there would be new arrivals from whom it was possible to glean some news about the outside world. The guards never spoke to them.

All the prisoners were so-called "black folk": small shopkeepers, artisans, clerks, cabmen, and beggars. The Secret Chancery drew far more important fish into its terrible net, but those were housed in separate cells.

It was indeed a strange and grim world for Peter to learn. Those fifty-odd men and women, thrown together by harsh injustice, formed a community of their own, and the woman, who promised Peter that he would be looked after, was their leader.

Everybody called her Aunt Nastia. She was small, shriveled, elderly. She never raised her voice, lost her temper, or fussed. She was never idle. When the niggardly light ebbed away, she sat in her corner, the knitting needles clicking in her bony roughened hands. By daytime Aunt Nastia kept herself at everybody's disposal, smoothing out the inevitable blisters of the daily rub, supervising over the fair distribution of food, heating soup and water, seeing to the replenishment of the stove, looking after this, that and the other, never meddling unnecessarily, but always near at hand whenever despair or anger threatened to add to the day's burden. She did everything as quietly and assuredly as though she were still in the tiny house behind her bakery and not in a noisome dungeon of Taganka.

From the first day Aunt Nastia was a friend to Peter. She arranged his pile of straw next to her own, cut his hair, did not wring her hands over his bruises but spread some ointment on them, washed his tattered smock and found a spare tin pannikin and a wooden spoon for his use. She made no comment and asked no questions. Only toward the evening when both of them were crouching by the open doors of the stove and Aunt Nastia saw tears welling up in Peter's eyes, did she say:

"Now no sniveling here, lad. Else you might start beating your head against the wall."

Peter dared not tell her that all her rough kindnesses carried his thoughts back to a home he could not bear to remember.

Having settled Peter, Aunt Nastia began telling him about the way of life they led.

"As soon as we hear the guards' boots on the stairs we all stop talking. What use is it for anyone to get a beating? But they come twice a day, and that's easy to remember." Aunt Nastia nodded toward a remote corner. "That's where the sick lie and I do what I can for them. But you keep away from that corner, see? We feed twice a day—victuals would not run to more, but God is merciful, there is no need to starve, lad."

Peter listened. He asked no questions. When Aunt Nastia stopped, he curled up and fell asleep.

It was hard enough by daytime. But the nights were worse. The doors of the stove would be closed tight to preserve the warmth. The place was pitch dark. Some talked in their sleep and screamed sometimes if a nightmare gripped them. Others kept awake and groaned from time to time. A shout would wake Peter and make him sit up, terrified of whatever the darkness hid from him.

Even by daytime there would come ugly moments when quarrels broke out now in one corner, now in another. Aunt Nastia would wait for the row to reach a certain pitch. Then she would shuffle across, her arms akimbo, and say sharply:

"Now that is more than enough, you, Karp, and you, Sidor. Does either of you want a taste of the guard's whip? Enough, I say—"

And the upraised fists would fall down and the violent voices sink to thick mutterings.

But it took Peter quite a time to be aware of such incidents. He remained lost.

One evening—it must have been in the summer—because light lingered for quite a while after supper, Peter told Aunt Nastia about the letter to the Tsarina.

The old widow listened. She made no comment. She pulled at the frayed gray rag which served her for a kerchief and said conversationally:

"And they put me here because of mentioning the high taxes to a German in my bakery one day—"

"What is a German?" Peter wanted to know.

"A man not of our nation. An infidel—"

"A devil then?"

"Well, first cousin to one, I should say."

Silence fell between them, and then Aunt Nastia said almost casually:

"Fancy you, a peasant lad, wanting to learn your

70

letters! Ah, son, you would have been in clover if Tsar Peter were alive. He would have got someone to teach you—"

Peter wished he might speak about his encounter with Tsar Peter's daughter. But that remained a secret never to be broken by him. Almost involuntarily his fingers brushed against the tiny icon on his chest, and Aunt Nastia saw the gesture.

"Your Mum's blessing, I reckon," she said, and Peter nodded.

The great thing happened a few days later. It was after dinner, and everybody felt so cheerful that a few voices were heard singing here and there. Merchants' wives having brought a generous dole in honor of a feast, the prisoners had had meat and mushroom pies, pickled herrings, and apples for their meal.

In their corner Aunt Nastia and Peter sat quietly. Suddenly she stopped knitting.

"Lad," she asked, "what is it that made you want to learn your letters and all?"

"Well," Peter muttered.

It was hard to explain. Words would not come, and after a bit he gave it up, but the few clumsy sentences seemed to satisfy Aunt Nastia. She got up and shuffled right across the room to where a thin wizened old man was trying to shake down his pallet.

"Stepan," Aunt Nastia whispered, "they did not take your book away, did they?"

The little man turned and stared at her.

"No," he muttered. "I keep it well hidden under the straw."

"Bring it out, Stepan, and come over to my corner. That young lad is longing to learn. You can teach him."

"Me?" he staggered back a little. "But—but—"

"Nobody will know," Aunt Nastia went on urgently. She had made up her mind. Old Stepan had his book and knew his letters, but he kept shaking his tousled head and screwing up his red-rimmed eyes. He kept the book well hidden, he mumbled, it was safer so. He had got to Taganka for having once spelled "Majesty" with a small "m." He had done with reading and writing, he mumbled, and there was neither paper nor ink in the dungeon. What could he teach the lad, he asked tremulously. Now if the boy wanted his boots cobbled, that was another matter.

"The lad has no boots," Aunt Nastia said patiently. "Get the book out, Stepan. Just show him the letters. He hasn't got hay in his head."

In the end, the old man delved under his pallet and brought out a dirty and tattered volume of *Sonnik*, the so-called Dream Book. Some of its pages were torn out. Aunt Nastia stooped low over the pallet. She thought that the print looked large enough. Old Stepan muttered:

"Here is a dream about water. It is unlucky to dream about water. But fog is worse—"

"Never mind water and fog, Stepan," she said. "The letters are all there, aren't they?"

"Now isn't that a fool's question? How could a book be printed unless all the letters were used, I ask you?"

"And how should I know, ignorant as I am?" she

retorted, steering the old man and his precious book across the room. Once in Aunt Nastia's corner, old Stepan threw a frightened glance at Peter, huddled against the wall, opened the tattered volume on a page with a crude engraving of a girl staring at a mirror and mumbled:

"Now watch my finger as it moves, boy. See, this is a big 'A' and there is a small 'a.' "

Peter held his breath. A big 'A' and a small one . . . Were there two letters inside each, and how many were there altogether? He dared not ask. Obediently he watched the old clerk's dirty gnarled forefinger move along the line. The big "A" was a bit difficult to remember, but the small one seemed easy enough—as round as a tiny pea with a little tail half-tucked in.

Before daylight faded, Peter had held the tattered book in his hands and had learned the first two letters of the alphabet. His voice shook when he tried to thank the wizened little clerk.

The supper eaten, Peter lay very still. Aunt Nastia thought he had fallen asleep. She fumbled for her knitting. She thought of old Stepan. Certainly she would try and slip an extra slice into his platter for tomorrow's dinner. He deserved it.

Peter could not sleep. He had told Aunt Nastia about his letter to the Tsarina and his urge to get himself educated. To nobody had he ever opened the secret hidden at the back of the little iron frame. But that evening Peter was back in Makar's Wood, flinging the raspberries at the bear, riding pillion behind Princess Elizabeth and hearing her musical voice. She had said she would never forget his service. She had told him to keep it all a secret, and he had kept his promise.

Peter had no idea how long he had been at Taganka. Even the passing of seasons was not easy to mark now that he had no sky, no trees, no grass to look at. In the dungeon the people talked often enough about the outside world forbidden to them. The matters they discussed and the names they mentioned meant nothing to Peter—with one exception, and the exception was Princess Elizabeth. Nobody lowered their voices when they spoke of her. She stood for daylight during their night. Peter knew that the Tsarina, to whom he had written, was her first cousin and hated and feared her, that she lived in exile and in great poverty. He well remembered how shabby her clothes were and that she said she had no reward for him.

But now that he had started wrestling against the darkness of the mind, now that he had learned the first two letters of the alphabet, Peter felt that come what may, he was on the right way, and suddenly he asked:

"Aunt Nastia, have you ever seen Princess Elizabeth?"

"Why, yes, lad, several times here in Moscow. Ah, there is a woman for you! No pride in her for all she is the great Tsar's daughter. God is merciful—she will come into her own one day."

"When?" he breathed.

"Ah the Lord alone knows when." And Aunt Nastia turned to her knitting again.

That night, for the first time since his arrest, Peter fell asleep, a smile upon his mouth.

8 News
of Peter reaches
Malinka

All that time the peo-
ple of Malinka worked as hard as ever since the
seasons' unchanging demands made no allowances
for anyone's grief or loss. Corn was sown, cut,
threshed, and ground; the peasants' portion, once
tax and tithe were paid, came into the barns. Berries, roots, and mushrooms were gathered. Tax
collectors came and went. A very occasional peddler would turn up with his bundles of knives, pins,
combs, and tawdry ribbons. The little bell of the
church pealed asthmatically at the appointed times,
and Marfa went to all the services, her hair hidden
under a white kerchief in sign of mourning.

But Father Foma refused to have a requiem sung for Peter, no matter how often Zakhar and Marfa begged him to do it.

"The boy is alive. All shall go well with him." The priest had no other answer to give to Peter's parents.

They dared not ask how he knew. Tax collectors had nothing to do with the Secret Chancery. Peddlers came from Kaluga and had little more than local gossip to tell Malinka, and there had been no news from Moscow all through the winter and the spring. The storm of her grief over, Marfa never cried again. Nor did she smile, or sing.

With the spring floods gone, the village began getting ready for the busiest time of the year. One evening Zakhar, spent to the marrow, came home to supper. He had been in the fields since before dawn, and now he wanted nothing but food and sleep. But the narrow table was not set for a meal, and there was no sign of Marfa.

"Gone to fetch water," thought Zakhar, "but it's strange that I did not see her on the way home." He sat down on the trestle and kicked off his dusty sandals. Then, hunger stirring in him, he stretched his hand for the loaf on the shelf, cut off a hunk, and began chewing. Suddenly he noticed that Marfa's blue sarafan, her one and only tidy garment, was not hanging in its corner. He stared, hunger forgotten.

"Surely, she would never wear it to fetch the water," he thought. "Goodness, what is she about?"

When Zakhar saw that the boots were also gone, his bewilderment gave place to anxiety.

"Spring weather and all! Queen of Heaven, has she made off to Moscow? But she would not—surely—Father Foma promised he'd send another message as soon as the roads were settled—"

Just at that moment Marfa appeared. She wore the blue sarafan and the beads, but for the white kerchief she had a yellow one. There were traces of tears on her cheeks, but her eyes looked starry. She waited at the door for a second, and then ran and flung herself into Zakhar's arms.

"The lad is alive," she cried hoarsely, "in prison—but alive, alive!"

Zakhar led her to the trestle, made her sit down, and stroked her head.

"Now quiet, wife, quiet—"

But Marfa could not be quiet. She went on shaking and gulping, crying and laughing. Semen's wife had come at dinnertime, she said, and would she, Marfa, go and see Father Foma at once, it was very important, said Semen's wife.

"So, husband, I tidied myself up, and I ran like a she-hare, and there was Father Foma and a letter, husband, a letter, all the way from Moscow, brought by a merchant, Father Foma said, from Moscow," she repeated.

"Yes," said Zakhar patiently and went on stroking her head, but Marfa could not remember anything of the letter except that Peter was alive.

There was nothing for it except for Zakhar to put on his sandals again and make for Father Foma's. He found the old priest eating his supper out of a small bowl. He laid down the spoon on seeing Zakhar and his sunken eyes shone.

"We shall sing a proper Thanksgiving on Sunday,

neighbor," he cried. "Yes, yes, a merchant from Kaluga brought a letter from Master Ilya. You remember him?"

Zakhar nodded.

"Peter is still in prison. There has been neither trial nor sentence—but he is alive—and Master Ilya and his wife have been looking after him—taking victuals and clothing, too. God reward them! It is all in the letter." And Father Foma rummaged in a chest and brought out a large piece of paper.

"Never mind the words, little Father," Zakhar checked him. "You have told me. And that is enough—"

"But so much has happened since last autumn, Zakhar. Here we have spent our winter as usual—buried in a bear's lair! We have heard nothing. Tsarina Anna is dead." Here custom led the priest to cross himself. Zakhar chose to ignore the custom: that Tsarina, he thought, had gone to her judgment for the cruelty to his son, who had done her no harm.

"Is there a Tsar now?" he asked almost indifferently, "or another Tsarina?"

"There is a Tsar, a baby—"

Zakhar's eyes flew wide.

"How can a child rule? It makes no sense to me."

"His parents do it for him."

"And who are they?"

"The late Tsarina's niece and her husband, so the merchant says." And Father Foma sighed. "Both are German, Zakhar."

"And is that wicked Secret Chancery still at work?"

"The merchant thought so," replied the priest and did not add that his visitor had prophesied a grim future for the country with the hunt for mostly imaginary traitors on the increase and new prisons being built in Moscow and elsewhere.

A taut silence fell between the two men, and then Zakhar asked diffidently:

"Has Master Ilya seen the lad?"

"He does not say so, but food and things have been going to the prison all the time."

"And how long are they going to keep him? Ah, little Father, it is hard—him having done no harm and me all alone in the fields—"

"I know, Zakhar, but Master Ilya will do his best, and I know that we'll have the bell ringing for joy before I die, ringing for the boy's return."

"You have always been sure, little Father? Why?"

The priest shrugged. He was still certain of Peter's eventual release but he could not tell why he felt so certain.

It was good to know that his son was alive and that there were friends near at hand. The rest of the news seemed utter nonsense to Zakhar.

He came home and told Marfa about the infant Tsar. But she was quite indifferent to all the dynastic changes. She had her loom out of its corner and talked about a piece of cloth she would weave for Peter's coat.

"Father Foma will see to it," she said, setting the loom in place. "There is certain to be a peddler or a merchant here in the summer."

The next day when the sun was high up Zakhar sat down under a hawthorn bush to eat his dinner of pickled fish and bread; a thrush alighted on a branch of an elm nearby, and his song made Peter's father wipe his eyes.

"Ah, lad," he whispered, "is there a bird for you to look at? That is the season you like best—with the ice gone from the river and the soil stirring and much hard work to your hand . . ."

And somehow the food lost its savor for Zakhar.

The following Sunday the people heard the short thanksgiving service after mass, and they crowded outside and kissed Peter's parents on both cheeks.

"News never comes singly," Marfa kept telling them. "Now we'll just wait for the lad's return. God be thanked that they did not kill him." And she hurried to the priest's house with her offering of a round rye loaf. Back in her hut, Marfa rummaged under a shelf. She possessed a single tablecloth, a remnant of the modest dowry she had brought to Zakhar. It was of fine white linen, embroidered in red and blue cross-stitch all round the edges. She took great care of it and kept it folded in a piece of clean sacking.

That Sunday Marfa spread it on the table and fetched a sizable cabbage pastry out of the oven. She smiled at Zakhar, and he asked no questions. He knew that the tablecloth was being used to do honor to their son.

But neither of the parents knew how long they would have to wait for Peter's return.

9 The darkest hours at Taganka

"Well, Peter," mumbled old Stepan, "you have learned all your letters. I can see that. Pity I can't teach you to write, but there is not a piece of charcoal in the place, let alone pen and ink." He sighed. "Just let us run over the top line again, shall we? Spell it out letter by letter. And don't hurry—a book is not a pie in the oven."

Peter breathed deeply, took up the tattered book in his hands, and began:

"T-o-g-d-a- *togda* [then]."

Laboriously, letter by single letter, he got to the end of the line. The little clerk listened, his tousled head bent on one side.

"You are no fool, boy," he said at last. "Aunt Nastia knew what she was about. But what next, I wonder? Heaven have mercy on us all—" Stepan pulled at his matted beard and stared at Peter, his red-rimmed eyes almost tearful. "Here they threw you and me into prison, and I have taught you your letters. I am town-bred, I belong to Moscow, and you are a peasant, and what is the difference between us now? Both in the same leaking boat . . . Poor you . . . Poor me . . ."

He stopped, but Peter knew he was not expected to answer. Nor would he have known what to say. Always, the lesson finished, would the old clerk fall into a somber mood, complain of his own sad fate, and pity Peter. And always the boy longed to stop his ears or to move away, and he never did either.

He stayed where he was and listened to the sad gray monologue. He felt deeply grateful to old Stepan, but he also knew that he would not mind if he never met him again. Peter preferred Aunt Nastia, who was never sorry for him, never wailed about the future, and dealt with each day's matters calmly, unhurriedly, vigorously.

"As set as a star in the sky she is," thought Peter.

Old Stepan, his grievances given yet another airing, shuffled back to his own corner, and soon murky twilight descended on the place.

Soon enough shortened hours of daylight told them they were in autumn. Gradually, a change crept into the tenor of their days.

To begin with, there had been no new arrivals for some time. It meant that the prisoners in Dungeon

3 were utterly in the dark as to what was happening in the outside world. Somehow or other, the very time slowed down. If it were not for the daily dole of water, fuel, and food, they would have been cut off entirely, but it seemed an eternity from one guard's visit to another. Inevitably, strained tempers snapped. Quarrels broke out so frequently that Aunt Nastia found her hands more than full. Her authority among them still held, but it was certainly a weary job to check every outburst of backbiting and quarreling and not to let them burst into open fights.

And then Peter got ill.

He did not think there was anything the matter with him. He just did not feel like getting up, something of a languor all over his body. And then he started a racking cough.

At the very beginning Aunt Nastia had told him she did what she could for the sick folk and that it was little enough. Her medicaments were few and rather primitive. She had a small supply of green oil; she would warm a little of it in a saucer and rub Peter's chest every evening. She had also some roots and a bag of dried blackcurrants which, when boiled, made a soothing enough drink. Yet Peter's cough did not mend at all.

Soon it was winter, and a cruel winter it proved to be. They all took to crouching as near as possible to the great stove, but breaths of icy air kept rushing in through the latticed openings under the ceiling. Within one week two elderly men and one woman died in the night. In the morning, the guards took the bodies away. That same day death came for old Stepan, too. He went, the tattered dream book clutched in his bony hands, but by then Peter was no longer able to do his reading exercises. His cough was a bit better, but his weakness grew day by day. He lay there, his eyes closed, and Aunt Nastia's heart ached for him.

Early one morning they woke to the bells summoning free people to worship. At Taganka, they could not tell if it was a Sunday or a feast. The breakfast eaten, they all moved nearer the doors.

Outside all the bells were ringing. In Dungeon 3 they waited for the accustomed tread of hobnailed boots down the staircase. They heard nothing, and that morning no armed soldiers appeared to open the doors. The prisoners stared at one another, terror in their eyes. Were they utterly forgotten? Aunt Nastia said as loudly and firmly as she could:

"Now, neighbors, it may well be that the chaplain has fallen sick and they could not find another."

They heard her. Nobody answered. They waited.

Always, once the service was over, the guards would come in with the dole, the fuel, and the water. That morning nobody came at all, and Aunt Nastia's mouth went into a thin, grim line.

To the left of the great stove was a fairly large space, and a few trestles in it served them for a larder. The daily dole would always be varied both in quality and in quantity, and Aunt Nastia would usually contrive to have some food put aside "for the rainy day." Behind the trestles stood the six vats of water.

Now it seemed that "the rainy day" had come,

and Aunt Nastia with her two helpers turned to the trestles. The old woman remembered that they had enjoyed a lavish dole for two days running. None the less, her mouth went grim. There seemed just enough for one meal among forty-odd people. Aunt Nastia decided that the supplies would have to do for two meals. As to water, five of the vats were empty, and the sixth far from full.

"A third of a mug each," she thought, "but will even a third of a mug go round?"

She knew she could not tell.

Her back to the people, Aunt Nastia permitted herself a glance at the latticed apertures. They were so high up. There were no ladders. She did not think that even all the upended trestles, stood on top of one another, would reach them. Nor was there a single tool about to break those iron lattices. Should they all start shouting? But if, as she feared, the place was deserted, who would hear them? She had an idea that two vast courtyards separated the prison proper from the street.

Aunt Nastia forced her mind to consider the food again. A slice of bread, a small piece of fish and a third of a mug of water apiece, and the fish had better be warmed up. Here, however, her heart all but failed her. There certainly was not enough fuel to last the day through. They had stoked the great stove earlier in the morning. What was left of the pile of logs was not enough for a second replenishing.

"Queen of Heaven," she thought, "why, the poor lad will die of the cold—having learned his letters and all."

She was ready to do her best for forty-odd people. But all her inmost thoughts were with Peter, whose cough had not improved for all the blackcurrant cordials she had been giving him.

She turned and saw that they were all watching her narrowly—except for Peter, who lay on his pallet, his wide-open eyes looking at a lattice above him. There was not a shred of fear or anxiety in those eyes. Having looked at him, Aunt Nastia felt that some of her own courage was coming back to her.

"Come, neighbors," she invited them, in as steady a voice as she could manage, "I reckon the guards have fallen down a well. There is little enough here, but we'll make it do, God helping us. Here, Glasha, you are the eldest. Mind you carry your mug carefully . . ."

She knew she had won the first round. Nobody rushed to the trestles. Nobody grumbled. Nobody swore. They took the food silently and shuffled back to their pallets. Peter alone did not stir, and Aunt Nastia carried both platter and mug to him, and he managed a smile.

He dipped a small piece of bread into the water and ate it slowly. The water refreshed him, but he would not touch the fish. The flush on his cheeks made Aunt Nastia catch her breath.

When she had eaten her own portion, she got up and said loudly:

"Now, neighbors, let us all get together and talk quietly. God is merciful."

But the conference achieved little enough. Few had anything to say. A man suggested that some kind of a ladder might be made out of the trestles, but they had neither choppers nor hatchets for the job. Someone else wondered if they could break down the doors with their naked fists. That suggestion was received in silence. And Aunt Nastia realized that very few among them had the strength to shout.

"Lord have mercy," she murmured under her breath.

By the evening the last crumb was eaten. The stove felt cold to the touch. Aunt Nastia put her own coverlet and her straw pallet over Peter.

They never knew how they spent that night. The dawn found them half-frozen. Their throats felt like leather. Aunt Nastia, numb from head to toe, dragged herself nearer Peter and saw his eyes open. She stopped and gathered him in her arms.

"God is merciful, lad," she murmured over and over again, dimly conscious that no other mercy was left to them, and a light in his eyes told her that he had heard and understood.

Suddenly a terrific bang was heard from behind the grimly barred doors. It sounded as though not the guards but a whole army were streaming down the stairway.

Peter stirred. Aunt Nastia held him closer. Nobody spoke or moved. Peter could not speak. He thought: will they take us out before they kill us . . . ? It's winter . . . Shall I see the sky and snow again? He made the hardest effort in his life and smiled at Aunt Nastia.

10 Moscow's belfries come to life

It was a bitter December evening. Snow had begun falling in the early afternoon. The people of Moscow, their business done, were glad to retire behind shuttered windows and bolted doors. It was an evening meant for little else than hot food eaten comfortably close to the stove. The inner room in Master Ilya's house was pleasant indeed with a snow-white cloth spread on the table, logs merrily crackling in the big stove, candles glimmering in front of the icons in a corner and more candles on a brass bracket above a bench covered with crimson cloth. A fragrance of mint water and olive oil lingered about the room. Presently Matriona and the serving girl brought in the supper—a great bowl of steaming golden millet, pike baked with mushrooms, meat and onion patties, and a large dish of apple slices fried with honey and butter. The serving girl went. Matriona set a crock of mead on the table, straightened a dish or two, and called out:

"Supper, husband!"

A door opened, Master Ilya came in, crossed himself, and sat down to his meal.

Husband and wife ate in silence, and neither of them looked very cheerful. The year just passed had not been particularly easy for the parish clerk of St. Zossima's. Discontent was seeping into every corner of Moscow. New taxes and new restrictions kept pouring in from St. Petersburg. People were fleeced on the right hand and on the left, and even humble peddlers did not always escape the tax collector's net. The news from the north was anything but reassuring: the little Emperor's young mother was said to pour money on jewelry, clothes, and pleasure pavilions. She was regent-in-chief, but little was heard about her taking any active part in government matters. They said that she spent her days in dancing, reading French novels, and gossiping with her ladies.

But the spate of stories about the little Emperor's mother did not particularly interest Master Ilya. Since the death of the Empress Anna he had been hoping for different news, but the visitors from St. Petersburg could not give him any such.

"Well, yes," they would say, "Princess Elizabeth

is now with us. She is supposed to be on good terms with her cousins, and she dines and sups at the palace often enough. They don't stint her for money nowadays. She wears elegant clothes and has good horses. The guards regiments and all the common folk worship her. And that is about all we can tell you."

And that was not enough for Master Ilya.

"Doesn't she know the state this country is getting in? Surely, that must trouble her."

But the visitors merely shrugged. They had no more to tell him, they said again.

And there was Peter. Ever since hearing the story about the letter written by Egor, Master Ilya had felt himself responsible for the boy. Yet there seemed nothing he could do. He was indeed a parish clerk, but of what importance was his ancient and honorable office today with the whole country overrun by German fortune-hunters? He had been to Taganka prison often enough, and what had he to show for his trouble? That leather-faced governor with a name no Russian could pronounce would not even see Master Ilya. All the other officers were German too, and even the guards were recruited from some foreign regiment or other. Master Ilya and Matriona had been taking food three times a week and clothing, too, sometimes. Could they be sure that the poor lad was receiving any of their gifts?

Toward the end of the meal Matriona began complaining about a neighbor's dog.

"Barking all night he was, husband, and the moon is on the wane. A bad omen that, they say." She sighed, helped herself to some apple fritters, and then stared at her platter for a moment. "The frost is cruel tonight," she went on almost under her breath. "I can't bear to think of that lad at Taganka . . ."

"Take heart, wife," Master Ilya tried to comfort her. "I have never heard that they freeze people to death in those places."

"And what—" Matriona began when a bang on the front door startled them both. Eyes wide with terror, she leaped to her feet and threw both arms round her husband's neck.

"I'll never let them take you away—"

"Quiet, dear heart, quiet," Master Ilya whispered.

They waited. They heard the serving girl run down the passage. In a moment the door was flung open. Egor stood there, the fur cap pushed well away from his forehead, his eyes starry.

"Long live Elizabeth! She is our Empress at last—" he cried, sank down on the nearest stool, and sobbed for joy.

Husband and wife, all speech forsaking them, crossed themselves. Then Matriona stepped forward and shook the clerk by the shoulder.

"Come and eat," she commanded, "and then get your wits together!"

"Wait a moment, wife," Master Ilya checked her. "Is it true, Egor? Not just a rumor, or a trap set by the Germans?"

The scribe raised his head and rubbed his cheeks.

"Go to the Kremlin, Master Ilya. Then you'll know. You haven't forgotten that you sent me to the Metropolitan's lodgings with some paper or other? I found the whole place teeming with the news. All the bells in Moscow will be ringing at dawn. Prince Golitzin decided that the people had best be told in the morning—" Egor faltered, and Matriona urged him to come up to the table.

When he had fed, he went on with the story heard at the Kremlin.

"Nearly a week ago it happened—at night. Princess Elizabeth just drove to the grenadier barracks and said to the men that she was there in her father's name to ask for their service. They followed her like a man to the Summer Palace, and not a drop of blood shed anywhere, everybody swearing allegiance to her. I heard the couriers say it was just like Easter when the people heard, and they say that all the German snakes from the Secret Chancery will now be fleeing for their lives." Egor stopped when he saw Master Ilya rise from the table.

"Come on, Egor, we must get to the Kremlin together. Wife, get my sheepskins and snowboots. Put a candle into the lantern, Egor, and keep quiet in the streets, will you?"

They went. Matriona waited.

It was long past their usual bedtime when Master Ilya came back, having gathered most heartening news at the Kremlin.

"Why, wife, it is indeed a fine beginning to her reign! The Secret Chancery abolished and capital punishment done away with, too, and a general pardon to all prisoners, murderers excluded, to be proclaimed tomorrow."

"Husband," Matriona wept and kept crossing herself. "Is it all true? Well, then, it must be Taganka the first thing for you tomorrow morning.

The lad has no kin in Moscow and it is no fit weather for him to start for the country—"

Neither of them slept much that night. They sat by the stove in their bedroom, such a joy in their hearts that Matriona wondered if it was all a dream and if they would wake up and find themselves back within the grim and cruel reality they had known for so many years.

But with the first streak of dawn Moscow learned the truth when all the belfries in the ancient city broke into a triumphant peal. People jumped out of bed, leaped into their clothes, and made for streets and squares. Long before the crowds reached the gates of the Kremlin, the air was thick with shouting.

"God save our lawful Tsarina!"

"Long live Tsar Peter's daughter!"

"God bless our Elizabeth!"

Crowds heard the official proclamation, snatched at what food was carried about by peddlers, and embraced one another. The bitter frost forgotten, they danced in the streets. It was December. They thought they were in May.

But Master Ilya did not go to the Kremlin that morning. He made straight for the Taganka.

He knew no more than anyone else did in Moscow that a foreign-born official of the Secret Chancery in St. Petersburg had outraced the Imperial couriers by some forty-eight hours to give warning to all the prison governors and their staffs, who, aware that the people looked upon them as enemies, had fled for their lives, making for the Polish frontier to the west.

Master Ilya got near Taganka, but he could hardly elbow his way for the crowds which, having heard of the general amnesty, had rushed to free the prisoners. Jostled and pushed from side to side, Master Ilya was surrounded by men and women, their faces grim and their fists clenched. Ahead of him, furious voices all but drowned the noise of the kicks delivered at the huge barred gates.

"Open, you German dogs—everybody is pardoned—"

"You have no business to hold them prisoners—"

But the gates stayed closed.

Master Ilya went on inching his way forward. Pushing and jostling as hard as he could, he managed to get to the very forefront of the crowd, and then remembered a friend of his at the Kremlin saying that all the officials of the Secret Chancery would be scuttling for their lives now that the hour of reckoning had come.

Were they really gone, leaving the helpless prisoners inside? Master Ilya lurched forward and brought himself nearer to the great gates. The huge keyhole gaped at him. There was no key in it, and a blind fury welled up in the gentle and kindly parish clerk of St. Zossima's. If any man wearing the hated uniform had appeared at that moment, Master Ilya's hands would have been at his throat.

Three or four stalwarts were kicking at the gates with all their might, but the stout oak, reinforced by iron, would not give. Then Master Ilya spoke in a voice of such authority that the men stopped kicking and stared at him dumbly.

"Run all of you and get hold of a few crowbars and axes, too. We'll break through. We must and we shall!" He raised his voice and knew that the crowd was listening. "And those scoundrels will learn what it means to disobey the Tsarina's commands."

The men ran off. Presently crowbars and axes were brought. The gates were assaulted so furiously that they gave. A deep sigh rose from the waiting crowd. Another moment, and they all surged into the first of the two great courtyards.

They raced across and swept through all the vast rooms where but two days before the German-born governor and his army of servile underlings had been busily doling injustice to hundreds of innocent people. The crowd swept on, smashing tables, chairs, desks, and cupboards as though they were made of matchwood. They plunged down one passage and down another. Not a soul was to be seen anywhere.

Someone shouted hoarsely:

"We must find the way to the dungeons, folks."

Master Ilya turned and seized someone's arm.

"We'll need crowbars," he said hoarsely. "Those fiends must have locked every door before they ran away."

The place was so cold that he shivered in spite of his sheepskins. What would it be like down below, he thought with anguish, and tugged at the little doors of a stove—nothing but cold wood ash inside and all the windows were so thickly coated with ice that you could see nothing through them.

Crowbars were instantly fetched from the yard, and suddenly a hoarse shout of triumph rose up to the ceiling: some of the men had found the way to the head of a wide dark staircase.

"Stand back." Master Ilya never knew how he had the strength to make himself heard. "Fetch candles from that room in front. Bring that flint box, too—"

Moments passed and they seemed eternities. The grim silence of the prison caught at the crowd. Nobody shouted anymore. They crowded by the mouth of the stairway, not a word or a sigh among them.

Armed with crowbars, candles, and hatchets, the men began the descent, Master Ilya well to the front. There seemed to be no end to those steps. At last, the men stood in flickering candleshine, the great grim doors facing them. A thick iron bar, secured by an enormous padlock at each end, told its story.

The crowbars, wielded with a furious will, did their work quickly enough. The huge doors groaned once or twice and then gave with a deafening crash. For a moment Master Ilya and the others stood still—afraid of what they might find in the dungeon. Then, his shaking hand struggling to hold the candle, Master Ilya stepped across the great heap of rubble.

He had to peer very hard before he could make out a huddle of human figures in the well of the place. Not a sound came from them. Were they alive? Master Ilya shivered, and the men behind him kept very still.

"Good people." The parish clerk of St. Zossima's could not control the tremor of his voice. "You are all free. We are here to get you out." He paused and added urgently: "Peter, are you there? Peter, ah, Peter—"

It was the spoken name that brought those immobile figures to life. A deep choral sigh reached the rescuers. Then a woman's hoarse voice reached the people by the door.

"Ah, but God is merciful! Peter, ah, Peter, someone is calling for you—"

To the end of his days Master Ilya could not clearly remember what followed. The rescuers certainly ran forward. Someone helped him carry Peter up the stairs. All around people were laughing, weeping, swearing in anger that "the German fiends" had escaped them. But all Master Ilya knew was that, once across the two yards, he saw a baker's cart, and the baker at once reined in, and the thin half-frozen body was put into the cart, Master Ilya's sheepskins over the boy's shoulders. Somehow they reached the house with the blue pigeon over the door, and Matriona and the serving girl were there. What followed belonged to the women, their good sense and their gentleness.

11 Master Ilya
writes an important
letter

They were now in January. Peter felt much better, but they still kept him in bed. The window gave him a generous slice of the winter sky, and pigeons would be busily exchanging remarks on the windowsill. A smell of mint and crushed raspberries lingered in the little room, the serving girl having just brought him a drink. She never chattered, and Peter was glad of it. For words were still rather difficult for him to hear or to say. In fact, strange as it seemed, he felt as though he was learning afresh the use of his five senses. It was good and also just a little bit shattering to breathe good pure air again, to touch soft things again, to taste good food, to hear gentle voices, to open his eyes and be able to see clearly without having to peer into a murky half-light.

Peter was still confused in his mind. He did not quite know what had happened to set his face toward sunlight again. He understood that he was among friends and was no longer a prisoner, but he did not know what had brought him into freedom. Those last hours at Taganka had been so terrible that their impact could only be remembered in stray wispy details. Which, doubtless, was a great mercy. So Peter remembered Aunt Nastia moving slowly from trestle to trestle and bringing him a bit of bread and a morsel of cold boiled fish. Peter also remembered the extraordinary stillness which had all but turned the dungeon into a churchyard, the brief daylight going and all warmth from the stove thinning down until his teeth chattered and his limbs grew so numb that he wondered if he would ever again be able to move them.

But at Master Ilya's, Taganka was not even mentioned. Aunt Nastia had called several times to see Peter, bringing currant buns and cheesecakes. She never mentioned the prison—even though she wept as she looked at Peter. She talked about the bakery, her nephew, the price of flour and suchlike things. In spite of her tears, she did not disturb Peter. She soothed.

And everything else was just as soothing. Matriona and the serving girl looked after Peter. They washed him, combed his hair, rubbed him with warm oil, brought various cordials, spoke softly, and touched him gently. When the dark fell, there was the comfort of candles flickering in the corner where the icons were, and Peter's own iron-framed icon was still on his chest. He slept, woke, and slept again. Once on waking, he remembered that he had learned to read, and such a light came all over his face that Master Ilya, on entering the room, wondered if the boy could have seen a vision. But the old man would ask no questions.

Presently they decided that Peter could get up. They were now in February, and the old city was already beginning to get ready for Elizabeth's coronation in the autumn. Master Ilya had quite a lot to say about it all, and Peter's blue eyes shone as he listened. He said very little himself, and Matriona still watched him anxiously. Peter had apparently recovered, but he was as thin as a rake and very quiet, and she wondered if he would ever be fit again for the hard life in the country.

One afternoon Master Ilya and Peter were together in the parlor. Suddenly the boy stretched out his hand for a book lying on the table.

"Like me to read to you, lad?" asked the old man. "Well, it is a grand travel book—all about a man who sailed all over the world."

Peter blushed and whispered shyly:

"May I open it, Master?"

"Why, of course, but it has not got any pictures, lad."

The boy's blush deepened. His hands shook as he opened the heavy leather-bound volume. Nor was his voice very steady when he began spelling one word after another—letter by letter, slowly but accurately. Master Ilya gasped, leaned back in his chair, and stared in amazement.

"However did you come to know your letters? Why, I had an idea I might start to teach you as soon as you were really fit again. Peter, when and where did you learn your letters? And fancy you keeping it all a secret—"

Rather brokenly Peter told his host about Stepan and the book of dreams.

"Learned your letters in that dreadful place, did you?" Master Ilya said very slowly. "Well, well . . . Now, listen to me, lad. Egor told me all about that letter to the late Tsarina. Did those men who took you away from Malinka ask you who had written it for you?"

Instantly the blush gave away to pallor on the boy's face.

"They did," he stammered rather reluctantly and looked away.

"And what did you tell them, lad?"

"That I just could not call it to mind, Master. What else was there to say? I had promised Egor I would never tell."

Master Ilya said nothing but his mouth went into a grim line. He knew only too well what used to happen to people who would not answer questions put to them by the men from the Secret Chancery, and he realized that it was nothing short of a miracle that Peter should still be alive.

"What a grand lad," thought the old man. "Keeping his promise . . . And getting himself taught in that foul dungeon . . . Those devils must all but have beaten the life out of him . . . What a lad, God be good to him," and so engrossed was Master Ilya in his private thoughts that it was quite a few minutes before he realized that Peter was speaking and must have been speaking for some time.

". . . and so she told me to say nothing to anyone until she came into her own, and so I promised her, Master. Not even my old dad knows anything about it."

"Knows what?" Master Ilya asked.

"Why, about the bear, and the crimson oak and the raspberries and Princess Elizabeth, the Tsarina, I mean—"

"What are you talking about? What bear? And what has the Tsarina got to do with it?"

So Peter had to repeat the story right from the beginning.

"And I still have the little twig she had given me but, Master, I could never dare get near her now, could I? I mean now that she has become our Tsarina."

"Well," said the parish clerk of St. Zossima's, "she must certainly be very busy . . ."

Peter sighed and put the book back on the table. Presently the serving girl appeared to get things ready for a meal. Neither the Tsarina nor the bear in Makar's Wood were mentioned during supper. Later, the evening prayers said, Peter went to bed, and Master Ilya sent the servant to fetch Egor from his lodging down the street.

"But, husband, it is Sunday—" said Matriona.

"I did not think it was Monday, wife," he replied. "And when Egor comes, see to it that nobody disturbs us."

Egor came and Master Ilya at once took him to the little office at the back of the house.

"You owe your very life to Peter," he said gruffly. "Those fiends asked him over and over again who had written that letter for him, and he kept saying he could not remember. And he has learned his letters there at Taganka when he never knew if he would see another sunrise. Now, my friend, what do we do? Once the spring floods are over, he must be sent to the country and see his parents. They will have had my message by now and they know all is well with him, but is it right to have him labor in the fields all his life?"

Egor shook his tousled head.

"Hardly, Master, but what can one do? Heavens above, I could lay my life down for the lad—"

"He needs you alive rather than dead," the old man broke in sharply. "He can read all right but he can't pen a single letter—yet. Not a scrap of paper to be found in that dreadful place! And it is a marvel that he has not forgotten everything after his illness! He must be given a chance, Egor. It would be sinful to waste him. What a brain and what courage! Now, my friend, I know you are not as young as you were, and it is a long and tedious journey, but I want you to ride to St. Petersburg now before the spring floods burst upon us."

Egor staggered back.

"Me—to travel to the north? Master, I have never been away from Moscow and they all say the road fairly teems with brigands—"

"And a moment ago you wished you might lay down your life for the lad!" Master Ilya said dryly.

"Yes, and you said that he needed me alive rather than dead," retorted Egor.

"So he does, and do you imagine I would send you off all by yourself? I have good friends at the Kremlin and you will travel in good company. Once you get to St. Petersburg, you make for the Summer Palace. I know that the Tsarina receives petitions personally once a week—"

"Me—go to the Summer Palace?"

"Yes, once you have brushed your hair and coat and polished your boots. And, mind, you are not to look like a frightened hare with a wolf in front! I am going to give you a paper and you shall hand it over to the Tsarina. When you get back here," Master Ilya's voice rang very stern, "not a word to anyone, you understand? Now be ready to start the day after tomorrow. Everything will be in fair shape by then."

Egor nodded and went. To Matriona's bewilderment, her husband stayed alone in the office far into the night.

Master Ilya knew all there was to know about official documents, but the paper he labored at proved no easy task. A document it might well have been called, but it was a document informed with life, warmth, and earnestness from the first line down to the last. Worded with the utmost economy, it covered no more than one foolscap sheet, but everything went into it: the bear, the raspberries, the crimson oak, Peter's letter to the late Tsarina, his thirst for "enlightenment" so that he might become useful to his own kind, his arrest, his loyalty, courage and iron perseverance and, finally, the promise made by the Tsarina that a reward would one day be his.

Master Ilya made several rough drafts before he dared to start writing the fair copy. It was well after midnight when he came to sign himself "your Imperial Majesty's most humble and unworthy subject," the only touch of formality in the letter. His signature written, the old man reached for a stick of red sealing wax.

"Let the good Lord see to the rest," he murmured, "but I hope and believe that the Tsarina will understand."

12 Once more
the bells of Moscow
ring

gor was gone, Master Ilya saying casually that he had sent his clerk to see about some business connected with St. Zossima's, and everybody accepted it readily enough.

Meanwhile, Moscow once more settled down to the habitual daily pattern. Yet this carried a subtle change. Over and above the preparations for Elizabeth's coronation, there was a deep sense of satisfaction that the hated aliens had gone. Every traveler from St. Petersburg had the same story to tell: the young Tsarina was surrounded by men and women of her own country.

Peter, his health and strength returned, was not idle. He helped Matriona about the house, looked over some books, and was learning penmanship; "calligraphy," Master Ilya called it, but the long foreign word did not come easily to the boy's lips. Nor were his first efforts particularly happy. He wept over the mess he had made of the first four letters of the alphabet.

"Now then, lad, a pullet is not hatched the day the egg is laid," Master Ilya tried to comfort him.

March came, and the old man waited for Egor's return from St. Petersburg. Matriona, of course, did not share her husband's impatience since she was ignorant of the cause, and once she reproached him:

"It almost looks as though you will be glad once the spring floods are over, husband. Well, I would much rather they did not come so soon. I shall miss the lad—as dear to me as though he were my own son."

"He is also dear to me," the parish clerk pointed out to her, but she shook her head.

"He may well be, but you don't seem to care much. Once the boy has left for Malinka, why, we might never see him again."

"Spring floods have not started yet," was all Master Ilya had to say. Peter, of course, was not in the room during that conversation, and neither husband nor wife suspected the fearful inward struggle he was going through. He had made no secret plans about going to the northern capital to ask for the reward the Tsarina had once promised him, but a strange flame kept burning in Peter's thoughts, and he was afraid of it. He longed to see his parents again and yet he knew that he had no great desire to settle down at Malinka. He seemed all divided within himself and that made him very unhappy, and it worried him that he could not open his mind to Master Ilya.

Then Egor was back. No sooner had he entered the house than the old man hustled him into the office at the back.

"Well, then, tell me all about it—"

"Oh, Master," Egor gulped and mopped his forehead, "I can tell you one thing—the Kremlin is nothing to the Summer Palace."

"I did not send you to look at buildings," Master Ilya said sharply. "Did you see the Tsarina?"

"Yes, Master, that is—from a distance. We were all told to stand by the doorway, and a gentleman in red velvet came and he carried a large silver tray. We were told to put all our papers on it, and the gentleman went up to where the Tsarina sat and he knelt, and she took all the papers from him, and we were taken into another great hall and given much good beer, four meat pies apiece and some apples." Here Egor paused to draw a breath.

"How many of you were there?"

"Oh, quite a crowd, Master. I was in such a state—I could not count them."

"Well?"

"Then another gentleman all in green velvet came out to us and said we were all to go home and the Tsarina's Majesty will deal with all the matters. And out we went, everybody being most civil to us."

"Now we'll wait," said Master Ilya. "God reward you, Egor."

Soon spring burst upon the country and roads were impassable. Some of the low-lying parts of Moscow near the banks of the Moskva and the

Yaouza were flooded. Then, all too soon, as it seemed to poor Peter, the waters started falling back. One evening after prayers, when he had already gone to bed, Matriona said to her husband:

"It will be the country road for the lad soon enough, won't it now? Well, we'll send him off honorably. Two new smocks Lenka and I have made for him and two pairs of breeches, too, and a few other things as well. But, dear husband, it will be hard to see him go—"

"Wait till it happens," Master Ilya replied.

"Why, I suppose in two or three days," sighed Matriona. "I have heard folk say that the road to St. Petersburg is quite clear by now."

The very next morning Moscow woke to the pealing of every belfry. Soon enough the people learned that the young Tsarina was in the city at the Kremlin Palace. She had arrived, it appeared, quite secretly, with just two ladies and a few grenadiers in attendance.

Master Ilya's household was at breakfast when they heard the news. Peter's face went a wild crimson. Egor nearly choked himself with a piece of bread. Master Ilya sprinkled so much salt over his porridge that he could not eat it. His friend, a portly deacon from the Metropolitan's household at the Kremlin, pleased at having startled them all with his news, asked Matriona for some beer and went on importantly:

"The Archdeacon was there when the Tsarina arrived, and didn't she laugh? Nobody recognized her at the city gates. She told the Metropolitan that she wanted to spend a few days in Moscow— quietly. She is going on to Petrovskoe—just a breath of country air, and—" The deacon smiled and sipped his beer when suddenly Master Ilya saw two men in court uniforms dismount at the door. He leaped to his feet. All the others turned toward the windows and within an instant all was wild confusion. Matriona wept, the deacon gasped, Egor started to tremble, and Peter's face went a chalky white. Lenka, the serving girl, dropped the butter dish, and Master Ilya reproved her. Nobody else seemed to have a voice left.

What followed was like a swift blurred dream. The door opened. A gorgeously uniformed man came in, bowed, and delivered the imperial command for Peter to be brought at once to the Kremlin Palace. Matriona staggered to her feet.

"The lad has done no wrong," she cried out and her husband said sternly:

"Don't talk nonsense, wife. Get the boy ready—"

Bewildered, Matriona looked at the serving girl.

"Never you mind the butter dish," she said shakily. "Run upstairs and fetch one of those new smocks and—"

The man in the green and gold uniform bowed again. None of it was necessary, he said politely, the boy was to come in the clothes he stood up in. Peter's smock and breeches were clean enough but they carried a patch here and there, and his sandals were shabby. But he was so frightened that all speech left him. He stood there, looking now at Master Ilya, now at Egor. He dared not look at the man in the green and gold uniform and he wished that the floor might sink deep into the earth and hide him. The Tsarina's messenger said kindly:

"Don't look so scared, lad. I reckon this will be a great day for you."

Peter heard but he could not answer. In a trance, he followed the man in green and gold, and he never remembered what happened on the way to the Kremlin. He never saw the Red Square, the entrance to the palace, the broad blue-carpeted stairs, the vast halls through which he was led. He wondered if he was asleep. . . .

Then someone told him to stop. He stood, his head bent, and from no great distance he heard the musical voice he had never forgotten:

"Well, you would not come to me, and so I had to have you fetched to give you the reward I had promised."

Then Peter dared greatly and raised his head. The young Empress Elizabeth was sitting in a great chair covered with crimson velvet. She wore a magnificent gown of lilac satin and there were jewels in her hair and at her throat. But the dark blue eyes looked just as kindly as he remembered them. The beautiful mouth was smiling, and Peter fell on his knees.

"Oh, mistress," he gasped and was silent.

"Isn't there something you would like me to give you?" He heard the caressing voice, and he knew that there was, but he could not speak of it, and he gulped.

"A—a harrow—" he brought out at last.

"Only a harrow? But it does not seem quite enough for the service you rendered me. Why, that bear might have done me great hurt—"

"And—or—a plow," Peter ventured, "or—or—a cow perhaps—"

"A plow and a cow," Elizabeth said. "Surely, there should be more—"

Peter thought hard. Her kindliness, her smile, indeed all about her, made him wonderfully at ease. He knew that there was something else. He must not forget his mother or poor Mashka, who had hardly been in his thoughts for such a long time. He supposed a good cloth sarafan would do for his mother. What had he promised Mashka long, long ago? Beads and a blue kerchief? Peter gulped again and made himself mention the sarafan, the beads, and the kerchief.

Elizabeth asked:

"Is there anything else?"

"N—no, mistress," he stammered.

The Tsarina glanced at a gentleman in red velvet standing a little behind her chair.

"Make a note of all those things," she ordered and looked at Peter very hard. "All of it is for your parents, isn't it?"

"Yes, mistress—"

"What about yourself?"

His cheeks burning a wild crimson, Peter stayed dumb.

"Well, then," said Elizabeth, "it seems that I must choose your reward, Peter. You must go and see your parents first. And then you'll come back. You will be going to school—I need boys like you to serve me and my people."

She stretched out her hand. Peter seized it in both of his. He should have kissed it, but his hot tears fell over the Tsarina's fingers. She smiled, got up from her chair and, stooping, kissed Peter on both cheeks.